**Trent followed Blakely
to the kitchen, eager to
ease the tension between them.**

He found her frantically wiping the stovetop when he entered. "Anything I can do to help?"

Halting midwipe, she hesitated before finally turning around. "Um…" Eyes wide, she bit her bottom lip. Something he found sweet.

She looked away. "Act____ _____ _stin's job to set the table."

Unwillin_ _____ _____ _____ _pped closer, el__ _____ _____ ____ _mained between t__ ___

"He's a gre__ ___ __kely. You've done a fantastic job.

She glanced up at him, her eyes glistening with unshed tears. "Thanks."

At the table, he clasped Austin's hand, then offered Blakely his other. The softness of her touch sent a wave of awareness through him. And, for a split second, it was as though they were a family.

Dreams he'd tucked away long ago drifted to the surface. Could he still have the one thing that had eluded him all his life?

MINDY OBENHAUS

always dreamed of being a wife and mother. Yet as her youngest of five children started kindergarten, a new dream emerged—to write stories of true love that would glorify God.

Mindy grew up in Michigan, but got to Texas just as fast as she could. Nowadays, she finds herself trapped in the city, longing for ranch life or the mountains. When she's not penning her latest romance, she likes cooking, reading, traveling and spending time with her grandkids. Learn more about her at www.mindyobenhaus.com.

The Doctor's Family Reunion

Mindy Obenhaus

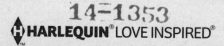
HARLEQUIN® LOVE INSPIRED®

Recycling programs for this product may not exist in your area.

™ LOVE INSPIRED BOOKS

ISBN-13: 978-0-373-87840-6

THE DOCTOR'S FAMILY REUNION

www.LoveInspiredBooks.com

Printed in U.S.A.

And we know that in all things God works
for the good of those who love him, who have
been called according to his purpose.
—*Romans 8:28*

For my family. Thank you.

Richard, you gave me the courage to follow my dream and cheered me on every step of the way. You are my best friend, my rock, and I will love you forever.

Amy, Rachel, Danielle, Ryan and Michael,
I love you all more than you will ever know.
Never give up on your dreams.

Jesus, my Lord and Savior, without You, I wouldn't have had a dream to chase. May it be for Your glory.

Acknowledgments

Becky Yauger, writing partner extraordinaire. Girlfriend, I couldn't have done this without you. Thank you for understanding how my brain works and for putting up with countless phone calls, emails, texts and IMs. We did it!

Many thanks to Ted and Betty Wolfe, owners of the Ouray Comfort Inn, for your friendship, hospitality and for answering a multitude of questions.

To Bob and Brandy Ross, owners of Switzerland of America, aka the little blue building on Seventh Avenue. You were my inspiration. Thanks for letting me hang with you guys. Your attention to detail shines through in all you do.

Thank you to all my writer friends who helped me along the way—Lisa, Lindi, Lena, Patty, Julie, Lynne, Kellie, Ruthy, Missy, Christy, Marilyn, Lee, Betty and Jackie. Your input, no matter how large or small, helped get this story where it is today.

Thank you to my mother-in-law, Helen Obenhaus, for introducing me to Ouray.

Melissa Endlich, you are the editor of my dreams. Thank you for believing in me.

And to the agent of my dreams, Tamela Hancock Murray, thank you for your support and encouragement.

Chapter One

Blakely Daniels' world had turned upside down.

Literally.

Her gaze darted throughout the cab of her tour vehicle, her breath ragged. Three tons of metal groaned around her, protesting against the copse of aspens that had stopped their free fall. The splintered windshield resembled a complex spider web and the indented driver's door pressed against her leg.

Head throbbing, Blakely squeezed her eyes shut, trying to get her bearings. She'd been driving these mountain roads since she was a teenager. Yet here she sat—rather, hung—who knows how far below the cliff's edge, her pickup in ruins.

How could she have made such a dangerous miscalculation? Praise God she was alone. She didn't even want to think about the outcome if she'd had a truckload of guests.

A pungent odor touched her nostrils. Her eyes flew open.

Gasoline.

She had to get out of here.

Now.

Thanks to the seatbelt's taut hold, she dangled precariously. Her ponytail swayed in front of her like the pendulum of the clock in Gran's living room. Traffic on these old mine roads this time of year was few and far between. So unless someone happened along…

God, I really need Your help. I know You already know that, but if You could please show me what to do.

Slipping a thumb under the satiny webbed fabric that held her captive, she moved her hand upward until she reached the harness. Her grip tightened as she wiggled, willing her back against the seat, trying to make herself as small as possible. Then, bracing one hand against the roof, she fingered the red button.

One. Two.

Oof!

Pushing up on all fours, she crawled across the soft gray fabric that lined the top of the cab and took hold of the latch on the passenger door. Because the truck rested on an incline, opening the door vertically would take all the effort she could muster. Pulling on the handle, she pushed with her shoulder but the door refused to budge.

She peered through the window. The sight of crumpled metal made her heart sink. She could only pray the damage wouldn't impede the window's descent. If so, she'd have to break the glass.

With the odor of gas growing stronger by the second, she hit the switch and the window disappeared into the door.

Thank You, Lord.

Blakely pushed through the opening.

Grasping at roots and spindly limbs, she clawed her way back up the steep slope. Cold mud seeped through her jeans, chilling her to the core.

Thirty feet later, she hoisted herself over the edge and stumbled across the narrow strip of road. The late morning sun warmed her face as she drooped against the wall of rock and filled her lungs with mass quantities of fresh spring air.

The untouched beauty of Colorado's San Juan Mountains

spread in every direction. Still adorned with their winter white, the jagged summits splayed across a pristine blue sky.

She rinsed her hands in a steady stream of run-off that rained down the face of the mountain before retrieving her phone from the pocket of her denim jacket. She unlocked the screen to see her favorite nine-year-old smiling up at her from the device, his big brown eyes alight with excitement.

For nearly ten years her greatest fear had been losing her son. At this moment she couldn't help wondering, what if Austin had lost her?

She glanced down at her bright pink tour vehicle, unable to stop the tears trailing down her cheeks. Who would take care of Austin if something happened to her?

Using the sleeve of her jacket, she wiped her tears away as she dialed Dan Carthage. Her mechanic and part-time guide would know what to do. "Please, please be there."

One ring. Two. Th—

"Hello."

"This is Blakely. I need your help."

Forty-five minutes later, Dan's Toyota SUV rounded the bend. But he wasn't alone.

Surely he hadn't brought her grandmother. The old girl would be beside herself if she saw the wreckage.

Dan, who was more family friend than employee, bolted from the SUV and hurried to meet her. "Are you all right?"

"Yeah." She gestured toward her 4x4 pickup that had been specially outfitted to carry up to nine passengers in open-air comfort. "It's the truck I'm worried about." Memorial Day weekend was just a little over a week away. The kickoff of the high season. The loss of a vehicle would mean fewer tours. Fewer tours generated less income. Income she counted on to pay the bills.

Ross Chapman would have a field day with this. Only a couple of hours ago, her rival had offered to buy Adventures in Pink.

Talk about nerve. Granddad started this company thirty-five years ago with a dream. A passion for sharing the splendor of these mountains with others. And he left Adventures in Pink to her. She couldn't imagine selling.

Dan let go a low whistle, distracting her from thoughts of Ross Chapman. "You walked away from that?"

"Piece of cake." Glancing over her shoulder, she watched as the other person—tall, dark and definitely not Gran—rounded Dan's vehicle.

Oh. My.

She blinked twice, her pulse racing once again.

His dark brown hair was shorter than she remembered, but those root beer eyes that had haunted her dreams for longer than she cared to admit hadn't changed one bit.

Tugging at her jacket, she crossed her arms over her chest. "What are *you* doing here?"

"Blakely...." Dan dragged out her name as though she'd embarrassed him. If he only knew. "I'd like you to meet Dr. Lockridge. I was at the doctor's office in Ridgway when you called. He offered to come along and help."

Of course, he did.

"Hello, Blakely."

She visually traced the outline of his face, the high cheekbones, his lazy smile. The last time she heard from Trent Lockridge he was in Albuquerque, riding off into the sunset with someone else. So he'd made it through medical school after all.

"You two know each other?" Dan's gaze flitted between them.

"It's been a while, but yes." Trent's scrutiny had her feeling like a disfigured bug under a microscope.

No telling how many kids he and his wife had now. Probably a whole houseful. Aside from becoming a doctor, Trent's greatest dream had been to have a family.

Looked like he'd gotten everything he ever wanted.

Jutting her chin out, she said, "I'll ask you again. *What* are you doing here?"

His stare faltered as he toed an embedded rock. "I thought Dan explained that. I work at the clinic."

"Since when?"

He looked at her now. "Since Monday." Was it her imagination or did Trent's shoulders drop a notch?

"Well, you're not working on me." Simmering anger and more what-ifs than she could count propelled her toward the SUV. A few swift steps into her escape, though, her head swam. Flashes of white light darted through her vision. She tripped.

"Easy." Strong hands grabbed her by the arms and kept her steady until she regained her wits. When she did, she quickly extricated herself from Trent's grasp.

"Looks like somebody's had a little too much excitement." He turned to Dan. "Let's get her to your truck."

To her dismay, they flanked her, wet gravel crunching in surround sound. Her mud-covered jeans had begun to dry and were slapping against her legs like a sandwich board. Miserable. And oh so unattractive.

Dan opened the door and Trent offered his hand to help her inside. She ignored the gesture. The last thing she needed was help from Trent Lockridge.

"You probably ought to give her a once-over, Doc." Dan adjusted the brim of his faded Broncos cap. "Rose Daniels would have my head if I let anything happen to her granddaughter."

Great. Trapped between two wannabe heroes.

She settled sideways in the backseat, keeping her filthy duck boots on the threshold. "I'm fine."

"What were you doing up here anyway?"

"Checking out the four-wheel drive." Not to mention venting after Ross Chapman's visit. Still, with all the rain they had yesterday, she should have been on the lookout for rock slides.

"And?"

"Works just fine." She glanced over the edge. "Or did, anyway."

"Let's just be grateful you're okay." The sincerity in Trent's expression sparked something deep inside of her, but she stomped it out like a wayward ember on parched grass. After all, he was a married man. Along with a multitude of other things.

"He's right." Dan visually scaled the face of the mountain. "Things could have been a lot worse, regardless of how well you know these roads."

Focusing on her grubby hands, she picked at the dirt imbedded under what little fingernails she had. "How long do you think the truck will be out of commission?"

Dan shrugged. "Can't say until we get it back to the shop."

While Trent disappeared around the back of the vehicle, she slid the elastic band from her ponytail. "Were you able to call the wrecker?"

Dan nodded. "Promised to get up here as soon as possible."

"Good." She worked her fingers through the tangled tresses. "What do you think the odds are of us keeping this little faux pas under wraps?" In a town as small as Ouray, news like this spread faster than butter on a hot griddle. Damage control would be imperative.

"I'll certainly do my part."

Blakely grimaced and sucked in a sharp breath. Pain radiated from a hefty lump on the left side of her head. Regrettably, Dan caught her pained expression, too.

He inched closer, his hazel eyes narrowing. "Uh, Doc, I think we've got a problem."

"It's nothing. Really. Just a little bump."

Trent pushed in front of Dan and set a small bag on the floorboard. "Why don't I have a look? Just to be safe."

"She's all yours, Doc. I'm gonna go check on the truck."

"Be careful," she said as Dan turned away. "The gas smell was pretty strong."

"Did you shut off the ignition?"

She cringed. That should have been her first instinct. She shook her head. "Guess I wasn't thinking."

"Gee, I can't imagine why." With a quick smile, Dan disappeared over the ledge, leaving her alone with the one person she never wanted, or expected, to see again.

Trent's broad-shouldered physique hovered over her now, so close she caught a whiff of his aftershave.

"Where does it hurt?"

She pointed to the side of her head, eager to be anywhere but in Trent's presence.

His fingers ran along her scalp, unleashing a flood of emotions.

"Ow!" She thrust a protective hand over the sore spot. But as Trent's deep-brown gaze collided with hers, long-suppressed memories escaped the darkened corners of her heart.

The heady rush of first love. The crushing blow of betrayal.

They say time heals all wounds. Evidently, eleven years wasn't long enough.

Trent recognized the hurt and trepidation in Blakely's blue eyes. Pain that had nothing to do with her head.

"You've got a goose egg the size of Mount Sneffels."

"Oh, it's not that bad." She waved a dismissive hand through the air.

"I'll be the judge of that." He pulled a penlight from his breast pocket. "Look straight ahead."

As much as he'd tried, Trent had never forgotten Blakely or that summer. When they finally said goodbye, they were counting the days until they could be together again.

Unfortunately, that never happened.

Instead, she got a phone call and news that he was marrying his ex-girlfriend.

The memory clamped around his heart.

If only it had been Blakely who carried his child instead of Lauren.

He flicked the tiny beam in and out of her line of vision. "Dan tells me you have The Jeep Company now."

"You mean Adventures in Pink."

He chuckled. "That's…interesting."

Her gaze remained fixed somewhere over his shoulder. "More than interesting. We're Ouray's premier adventure destination. And we've got the best maintained vehicles in town. Besides, real men aren't afraid of pink."

He pocketed the light again, his gaze drifting toward the ledge. "I don't expect you'll be using that one anytime soon."

Her shoulders slumped, her long golden waves tumbling around them. "Unfortunately."

He took a step back. "Without turning your head, I want you to follow my finger." He moved it back and forth, up and down.

"So…you live in Ridgway?"

"Ouray, actually." The picturesque town was what had enticed him to take the temporary job.

Her eyes widened. "With your family," she said more as a statement than a question.

He dropped his hand, wishing he could turn back time and erase the pain he'd caused Blakely. "My wife died two years ago."

She straightened. "What about your children?" She shook her head. "I mean, child?"

"Lauren miscarried shortly after we married." Then proceeded to inform him she wasn't interested in having children at all. Robbing him of the only thing he wanted more than becoming a doctor—a family.

"I see." Blakely's brow furrowed, her full lips pursed. A reaction he only wished he could interpret.

"Anything besides the dizziness I should be aware of? Any nausea?"

"No."

"Blurred vision?"

"No."

"So far, so good. Are your grandparents still at the motel?"

"Gran is. Granddad died last fall."

The news felt like a physical blow. "Bill was a good man." Without him, Trent never would have come to know Jesus.

"The best."

Memories took over, making him smile. "Quite the card, too. I'll never forget when he drove me up to Black Bear pass. Had me in stitches the entire way." He held open his palms. "Now squeeze my hands."

"What?"

"I need to test your strength."

"You must be out of your mind." Blakely hopped out of the vehicle, started toward the ledge, then turned, her blue eyes penetrating like a laser. "So how did you know I was here? Internet? Social media?"

"What? No. I had no idea you were in Ouray until Dan mentioned your name on the ride up here." After all, her dreams had been in Denver, picking up where her father's left off when his plane crashed. All she'd ever talked about was getting her degree and claiming the helm of BD Industries.

She kicked at a rock, sending it sailing over the ledge. "You must still think I'm the same naive girl you knew all those years ago. But come on, Trent, we both know how much you wanted a family. So why don't you admit the real reason you're in Ouray."

He'd always loved her fiery spirit. A perfect match for that strawberry-blond mane of hers. But apparently he'd lost his touch in their battle of wits.

"Blakely, what are you getting at?"

"Do I really have to spell it out?" She closed the distance between them, her face growing redder with every step. "Austin is *my* son. You chose not to be a father to him. So if you think I'm just going to let you waltz in here after ten years…"

Her words pummeled him like the boulders that fell from these mountains. Son? Father? Ten years?

His mind raced back to one special night almost eleven years ago.

It wasn't possible.

Blakely knew all about his childhood. How he'd been passed from one foster home to another, never knowing what it was like to be part of a real family. She was the only person he'd ever confided his longing to someday have that family. She would have told him he had a child.

Feeling as though a horse had kicked him in the stomach, he struggled for his breath.

"I have…a son?"

Chapter Two

Trent stepped outside his room at the San Juan Inn, the cool morning breeze making him shudder. Or maybe it was thoughts of the woman he'd run into on Camp Bird Road yesterday. The scorn in her eyes.

How could he have a child and not know it?

Unfortunately, Dan arrived back on the scene before Trent could get the answer to that question and so many more. But now, finding answers was at the top of his agenda.

He thrust his hands into the pockets of his faded jeans and wandered down Sixth Avenue. Nestled in a bowl of thirteen-thousand-foot peaks, Ouray waited in the shadows for the sun to top the Amphitheater. The unique setting of this tiny town captured his heart that long ago summer. Along with a certain strawberry blonde.

By the time August drew to a close, he had entertained thoughts of forever. Never imagining what awaited him back in Albuquerque.

He let go a sigh, his breath visible in the chilly morning air. God may have forgiven him, but sometimes the past crept in, reminding him what a lowly creature he'd once been.

Though You have made me see troubles, many and bitter,

You will restore my life again; from the depths of the earth,
You will again bring me up.

The verse from Psalm seventy-one had seen Trent through some of his rockiest days. Both before and after Lauren's death.

Growling echoed from his midsection. Perhaps some breakfast would improve his perspective. Not to mention a good cup of coffee. That weak stuff they served at the motel wasn't close to cutting it. Too bad Ouray didn't have a Starbucks.

Warmth bathed his back as the sun peered over the mountain behind him. He'd never tire of this scenery. The peace and tranquility it offered were what he longed for when he learned of the temporary opening in Ridgway.

He glanced at the Community Center where he'd once had the privilege of escorting Blakely to a dance. Sure, they'd been young—Blakely fresh out of high school—but the bond they'd forged that summer went beyond special. They "got" each other in a way no one ever had. Soul mates. Kindred spirits. With her, he'd felt accepted for the first time. Even loved. And he'd loved her, too.

So why hadn't she told him he had a child? More important, why did she seem to think he did know?

Raking his fingers through his hair, he prayed she and their son could one day forgive him.

At the corner of Main Street, he waited for a large motor home to lumber past. Once the exhaust dissipated, the most amazing aroma captivated his senses. He inhaled deeply, savoring the scent of roasting coffee beans. Lifting his gaze, he spotted what was sure to be his favorite new spot: Mouse's Chocolates & Coffee.

Maybe he wouldn't pine for Starbucks after all.

He hurried across the street.

"What can I get you?" A bubbly blonde, barely old enough to be out of high school, smiled behind the counter.

After eyeing the menu, he said, "How about a tall Americano?"

"We only have one size, sir. Sixteen ounces."

"That'll work."

Cup in hand, he paused at the corner. Less than a block away, the vacancy sign at The Alps Motel glowed red-orange. Apprehension kept his feet glued to the sidewalk. Were Blakely and his son there? Or did they live in one of the apartments over The Jeep Company—make that Adventures in Pink?

He wanted—needed—answers.

"Trent?"

Turning, he found Blakely's grandmother, Rose Daniels, smiling up at him. He couldn't help smiling back. The woman who'd provided him with many a meal that summer and more cookies than he'd had in all the years since had always held a special place in his heart.

"I was hoping I might run into you." Sincerity sparkled in her blue eyes. "Blakely mentioned you were back in town."

That must have been an interesting conversation.

"It's great to see you, Mrs. D." A motorcycle sputtered past, its engine mimicking the chug-chug of his heart.

"I hear you're working in Ridgway?"

"At the medical clinic. Yes."

"Wonderful." A wisp of white hair escaped her tight bun to dance about her round face. "Bill would have been so happy to know that you achieved your dream of becoming a doctor."

"I was sad to hear he's no longer with us. He was probably the greatest man I ever had the pleasure of knowing." Trent observed the rows of colorful Victorian buildings that lined Main Street. How he wished he could thank Bill for the impact he'd had on his life. A smile tugged at the corners of his mouth. Someday.

"Would you like some help with those?" He gestured to the green reusable grocery sacks that dangled from Rose's capable hands.

"That would be lovely. Thank you, Trent."

He gathered the trio of bags in one hand and started in the

direction of The Alps, making sure to abbreviate each stride so Rose wouldn't feel rushed.

"How long have you been back in Ouray?" She carefully maneuvered down the sloped sidewalk. No matter where you went in this town, you were either walking up or down hill.

"Since Sunday. I'm staying at the San Juan Inn."

"What?" She sent him a sideways glance. "Not The Alps?"

"Uh…" The muscles in his jaw tightened. The Alps had been his first inclination.

She nudged him with her elbow. "I'm teasing. The San Juan Inn is a wonderful choice."

Relaxing, he eyed the planters of red, white and purple flowers that graced the front stoop of the Daniels' home. The picket fence surrounding the tiny yard added an old-world charm to the beige two-story that also housed the motel's office.

Rose held open the gate, and he followed her to the door, his desire for answers getting the best of him.

"Tell me about my son."

The old woman looked bewildered for a moment before a proud smile erupted. "Austin is a good boy. Kind, friendly, active." She chuckled on the last word. "And he looks just like his father."

"I can't wait to meet him." He glanced down at a small patch of grass, emotion clogging his throat.

"You will."

"I promise, Mrs. D, I never knew. If I had…"

She laid a wrinkled hand on his shoulder. "Neither Bill nor I ever doubted you, Trent. We may not have understood, but we never stopped praying for you."

He studied the woman in front of him, who, even now, after everything that had happened, made him feel loved. So confident. Wise. Caring.

Somehow, he had to make things right.

She reached for the doorknob, turned it, but the door refused to budge. "Oh, this silly thing." She shoved one more time and it jerked open. "Bill had planned to put in a new one this winter."

Only then did Trent notice the weather-worn wood on the bottom half of the door. "Well, I'm pretty handy. If you're not in a big rush to get it fixed, I'd be happy to take care of that for you."

"Only if you'll let me pay you."

"I won't hear of it." He handed her the bags. "However, you do make the best peanut butter cookies I've ever had."

That earned him a grin.

"You can have all you want."

"So is Blakely at Adventures in Pink?"

"Should be."

He raised his coffee cup. "Wish me luck."

"I'll do you one better." She winked. "I'll pray."

"Thank you. And I'll be in touch about the door."

He headed down the alley across the street then eased left at Seventh Avenue. Two bright pink four-wheel-drive pickups with three rows of bench seats were parked in front of the familiar blue building, just waiting to introduce visitors to all these mountains had to offer.

The long narrow bench where Trent had shared countless conversations with Blakely and her grandfather still stretched across the front of the building. Trent had lived in one of the upstairs apartments along with a couple of fellows he'd dubbed Chaos and Destruction. His escape from the madness had been this bench, taking in whatever bit of history or insight Bill chose to impart.

Now, his heart hammered against his ribs as he opened the door and stepped inside.

A mural of Twin Falls was the first to welcome him, followed by a tiny dog with a high-pitched bark.

"Jethro."

The voice didn't belong to Blakely, and Trent was surprised

by the hint of disappointment that swept over him. He'd have expected relief.

Instead, a green-eyed brunette glared at the pup from behind the counter. "Don't mind him. He's all bark but no bite."

"That's okay." Trent knelt, holding out his fist to allow the animal to sniff. "You were just saying hello, weren't you?" He stroked the dog a couple of times then straightened, returning his focus to the painting. The attention to detail was so pronounced that he could almost hear the roaring waters and smell the Columbines and Indian Paintbrushes. And was that—he leaned closer—a marmot?

"Gorgeous, isn't it?"

He faced the thirty-something woman. "Yes. Yes, it is."

"Our owner did that." She leaned back in her chair. "She's quite a talented lady."

"Blakely." He'd recognize her work anywhere. Work that seemed to have improved with age.

"That's her." She cocked her head. "Are you a friend?"

"I'd like to think so." Even though Blakely might disagree. He approached the counter. "Is she here?"

"She's out in the shop. I'd be happy to get her—"

The telephone rang.

"Excuse me."

While the receptionist took the call, he roamed the selection of T-shirts, bumper stickers and other souvenirs near the front windows. What a great addition, as was the snack bar in the corner that boasted sodas, coffee and water. They'd really ramped up the old Jeep company.

The telephone conversation grew lengthy, and impatience got the best of Trent. After catching the brunette's eye, he let himself out the back door.

An acrid odor assailed his nostrils the moment he stepped into the garage. The place had more rubber than a tire store. Wheels were stacked five high throughout the space, with more lining the walls overhead.

The whir of an impact wrench cut the air. Blakely was out here, all right. But where?

Two pink Jeep Wranglers and a large red tool chest later, he found her.

Squatting beside a third Jeep, Blakely's movements were as adept as any pit crew member at the Indy 500. No sponsor-littered coveralls for her, though. She wore jeans and a T-shirt, pink, of course, with the company's logo in white lettering. Her hair had been gathered into a ponytail that trailed down her back.

His fingers twitched. He'd always loved her hair, the feel, the smell. Not to mention those cute freckles.

Something cold and wet touched his hand then, interrupting his reverie.

He looked down to find a golden retriever smiling up at him, tongue lolling out one side of its mouth.

Instinctively, Trent stroked the animal's head before returning his gaze to Blakely.

The noise stopped.

She pushed to her feet and moved toward a stack of tires, never noticing him.

He knew he should say something, let her know he was there. Instead, he just stared, still rubbing the dog's ears. The woman before him was prettier than the girl he remembered. But it was what was on the inside that had drawn him to Blakely. Strength. Passion. Loyalty. How could he have been fool enough to let something like that go?

Because you messed up big-time, buddy.

Wincing at the memory, he watched Blakely hoist another tire.

"Those things look heavy. You should ask for help."

She flinched but quickly recovered. "I'm pretty good at doing things myself."

Double meaning inferred, he was certain.

He perused the damaged tour truck in the next bay. Studying the wreckage, he shivered. *Thank You for watching over her, Lord.*

"You always did love being up here with your grandfather." He shortened the distance between them. "I'm not surprised he passed it to you."

Mounting the tire onto the axle, she all but ignored him, her shoulders rigid.

He came alongside her then, the retriever still at his heels. "How's the head?"

"Don't tell me you're here for a house call."

"No. Just curious." He gathered a bolstering breath. "I'd like to talk to you about my son."

Latching on to the hose that dangled from a reel overhead, she fired up the noisy power tool again, making conversation impossible.

Before he could figure out his next move, a young boy appeared through one of the open garage doors.

Trent's heart pounded when he saw the shock of dark hair that curled over the boy's ears and brow. His eyes were the color of coffee, just like Trent's.

He recalled how Blakely used to tell him his eyes were root beer colored and wondered if she did the same with Austin.

The boy was small for his age, but he'd grow out of it. For years, Trent had been the shortest one in his class. Then, almost overnight, he'd hit his growth spurt and surpassed them all.

The noise stopped when Austin touched Blakely's shoulder. "Can I go to Zach's house?"

Standing, Blakely sent Trent a warning glance before turning her attention to her son. "Did you finish your chores?"

"Yes, ma'am."

She smiled, eyeing the basketball in his hand. "I take it you two are planning to shoot some hoops?"

"Yeah."

Trent watched the exchange in amazement. The boy shared his mother's smile. They obviously had a good relationship.

And Trent liked that Austin had respect and manners. Back in Albuquerque, he'd encountered kids Austin's age who thought they could say or do anything they pleased without any concern for others.

"Will you be home for lunch?" she asked.

Austin was already out the door. "Yeah. Zach and his parents are going to Montrose at noon."

"Good. Ellie Mae told me she wants you to take her for a walk." She massaged the dog's head.

"Oh, Mom." He waved, trotting up the alley, bouncing the ball as he went.

Trent stared after him, his heart bursting with an emotion he'd never experienced before. Unequivocal and unconditional love for a boy he'd never even met.

Blakely watched after her son, then cut a fiery glare at Trent, pointing the impact wrench in his direction. "Don't think I'm buying this bit about you being here as mere coincidence. But if you think you're going to get your hands on Austin, you're crazy."

"How could you not have told me, Blakely? You of all people—"

"Is there a problem here?"

Oh, no. Please, not now.

Out of the corner of her eye, she spotted Ross Chapman at the rear of the Jeep Wrangler, scrutinizing her first, then Trent.

Despite the color leaching from her face, she turned Ross's way. "Not at all."

Neatly bearded with an ever-expanding paunch, the annoying Texan moved closer and extended his hand toward Trent. "I don't believe we've met. Ross Chapman." His crooked smile reminded her of a politician or unscrupulous salesman. Ever ready, usually insincere.

Trent hesitated before acknowledging the gesture and introducing himself. Apparently even he sensed the guy was a creep.

"Dr. Lockridge was just leaving." A stern glare accompanied her formal reference.

Straightening, Trent appeared to regard her with a challenge of his own. "Yes. I believe we're finished. For now."

He got points for knowing when to walk away. Then again, he was good at that, wasn't he?

Blakely tempered her anger and addressed her next problem. "What can I do for you, Ross?"

He moved in her direction, eyeing the battered tour vehicle. "Heard you had a little accident the other day. Wanted to make sure you were okay."

If he thought she'd believe that, the man was delusional.

"Good thing you weren't carrying a bunch of tourists."

She rested her elbow on a stack of tires. "You know, Ross, that's one difference in how you and I do business. To you, they're merely tourists. To me, they're guests."

"Call 'em what you want. We both rely on them to pay our bills." His gaze roved the truck again. "Word travels fast in a small town. Sure hope this doesn't hurt your business."

Panic and anger burned a trail from her belly to her throat. Still, there was no way she'd give him the satisfaction of losing her cool.

"I'm not worried." Willing her body language to follow suit, she shifted the power tool to her left hand and held out her right. "Thank you for your concern, Ross."

His green eyes narrowed, drawing his bushy eyebrows closer together.

Obviously, her reaction wasn't what he'd expected.

Good.

Ignoring her outstretched palm, he exited the garage.

Blakely turned back to the Jeep, feeling as though she might collapse. Her insides were as unsteady as a Tilt-a-Whirl. Would

Ross really slander Adventures in Pink? What if Trent tried to take Austin?

No. She wouldn't allow either one to happen.

Locking the impact wrench over a lug nut, she let it whirr. Tears stung her eyes. Her worst nightmares were coming true.

With the wheel secure, she rested her forehead against the black rubber. *I can't do this, Lord.*

How would she ever find her footing when everything kept crashing in around her?

She sniffed. She had to find a way.

Because she could not—would not—lose her son or Grand-dad's business.

Chapter Three

Trent wandered the streets of Ouray until the noon whistle pierced the air the way regret pierced his heart. Austin had been forced to pay the price for his indiscretions. Trent knew all too well what it was like to grow up without a father, and he had vowed no child of his would ever suffer the same fate. That's why he'd married Lauren in the first place. Even though he'd loved Blakely.

He meandered up the steep slope of Eighth Avenue, the roaring current of Cascade Falls drowning out all other sound. Too bad it didn't cover the turmoil thundering through him.

Hurt and anger were still at loggerheads over Blakely's decision not to tell him about Austin. Was it because she didn't want him to feel trapped? Or maybe she didn't find out until after he was married. Whatever the case, she'd kept him from knowing his son.

Guilt twisted his insides. He could only imagine the challenges she'd faced as a single parent. It couldn't have been easy, raising a child alone.

He plunked down on a boulder near the falls and watched the water plummet to the raging stream below. The turbulence mirrored his mood.

Sunlight sliced through a canopy of ponderosa pine and

aspens as giggles drew his attention to a couple of kids leaping from rock to rock.

"Stay away from that water," the mother warned her wayward children.

While his little sister complied, the young boy inched ever closer, an adventurous smile firmly in place. With a quick lunge, his father grabbed him by the arm and pulled him away.

"Come along, son. Your mother wants to get our picture."

Trent envied the scene. His life could have been so different. Full instead of empty.

I've decided I don't want children, Lauren had said after the miscarriage.

His dreams of a family shattered.

He felt a tap on his shoulder.

The kids' mother sent him a pleading look. "Sir, would you mind taking our picture?"

"Sure."

"All right, gang..." She herded her small family together, positioning them in front of the landmark. "This one's for the Christmas card."

"Cheese."

Trent returned the camera and trekked away from the happy family, wishing he could douse the ache for one of his own. Everything he'd ever wanted was here in Ouray. And he never even knew it.

"Slow down, girl."

A golden retriever careened toward Trent, pulling the dark-haired boy at the other end of the leash.

Austin.

Trent's chest thudded with anticipation as he bent to intercept the dog.

"Ellie Mae...." Austin moved closer, shortening the leash as he approached. "Sorry, mister."

"Ah, it's all right. We're friends, aren't we, Ellie Mae?" He rubbed harder.

The pooch sat at Trent's feet, tongue dangling, and continued to enjoy the affection.

"She sure likes you."

Trent savored the smile on his boy's face, the way it sparked his brown eyes. "She's a golden retriever. I bet there aren't many people she doesn't like."

"Yeah." Austin knelt beside the animal and stroked her back. A smattering of freckles dotted his nose and cheekbones—like Trent had at that age. "You were at my mom's shop."

"You're a very observant young man. I'm Trent."

"I'm Austin."

"I know. Your mom's an old friend of mine."

The boy's eyes widened. "Really? Did you know my dad?"

Trent recognized that gleam of expectancy. For years after his mother died, he'd held on to the hope of one day meeting his father. He wanted to reveal to the boy that he was his dad. However, he knew that wasn't necessarily what was best for Austin.

"What has your mom told you about him?" Bolstering himself for what could be an uncomfortable response, he focused on a couple of magpies vying for a scrap of bread.

"Not much." Austin shrugged. "Just that he loved me, but he had to go away."

The reply surprised Trent and pricked his conscience. At least Blakely had acknowledged him in some sense.

He inhaled the aroma of pine. "She's right, you know."

"So you do know my dad."

Trent's gut clenched. He wouldn't lie by saying no, but even if he said yes, would Austin perceive it as a lie whenever he did learn the truth?

"Do you think I'll ever meet him?"

Thankful for the reprieve, Trent said, "That, I can promise you."

Austin beamed.

"By the way..." Trent straightened. "How was the basketball game?"

The boy stood beside him now. "Too short."

"Bummer."

"Yeah."

Trent wasn't ready to relinquish these few precious moments with his son. "Well, I'm not doing anything. How about a game of one-on-one?"

"You mean it?"

"Sure. There's got to be a hoop around here somewhere."

"There's one at the park. Just down the road." Austin pointed in the direction of the city's hot springs pool. "I'd have to get my ball, though."

"No problem. Why don't you let Ellie Mae run you home, and I'll meet you at the park?"

"Awesome!"

As his son jogged away, Trent wondered how Blakely would react if Austin told her who he was meeting. He'd give it an hour. If Austin didn't show by then, Trent might have to pay her another visit.

The roar of the falls faded in the distance as he picked his way back down the rocky terrain, heading in the direction of Fellin Park. Obviously he and Blakely still had plenty to talk about. But one thing was for sure—now that Trent knew about Austin, nothing would keep him and his son apart.

Blakely was ready for a long soak in the motel's hot tub. Or maybe she'd sink into a bubble bath where she could be alone. Her body ached from lifting heavy-duty tires. Her mind reeled from worrying about Trent and Ross, her son and Adventures in Pink.

Plus, she had no idea what to fix for dinner.

She cut through the motel's front office, stopping to check how many guests were booked. It wouldn't be long before every motel in town would be filled to capacity, especially on the weekends.

"Gran?" She continued down the hall that separated the office and housekeeping areas from the main part of the house.

"In here, dear."

Jethro yipped, stopping when Blakely scooped the Yorkshire terrier into her arms. Ellie Mae nudged her hand, looking for some love of her own.

Blakely leaned against the doorjamb of the laundry room. The fragrance of spring-fresh fabric softener filled the air. "Hey."

"Hey, yourself." Gran smiled, pulling another load of white towels from the dryer. "You look beat."

"Nothing a good dinner and tub of hot water won't cure. Where's Austin?"

"Still at the park, I guess." Her grandmother halved then quartered a wash cloth and set the neat square on the stainless steel worktable. "He did tell you, didn't he?"

"Yes. I just thought he might be home by now."

"Well, if I know my great grandson, he probably ran into one of his friends. He's a good boy, though. He'll be home before dark."

"I suppose you're right." She nuzzled the soft fur on Jethro's neck. Gran was usually right. Blakely wished she could talk to her about Ross Chapman. But it would break Gran's heart. After all, she and Granddad had run two of the most successful businesses in town for almost forty years. Through good times and bad.

Now the season hadn't even started—her first as owner—and Adventures in Pink was already on rocky ground.

Shoving a stack of towels aside, Gran rounded the long table. "Would you prefer I fix dinner?"

"No, I'm just being whiney. You have enough to do." With Granddad gone, responsibility for the motel fell solely on Gran. Yet she never complained.

Blakely would do well to take lessons.

The bell dinged in the office.

"Putting on new tires today?" Her grandmother paused on her way out the door.

"How'd you know?"

Gran ran a thumb across Blakely's cheek, then held it up to reveal a black smudge. "It's written all over your face." Chuckling, she continued down the hall.

Blakely groaned. No telling how many people she'd talked with looking this way.

She set Jethro to the floor and shuffled toward the bathroom. "I am so ready for this day to be over."

This was the first time she'd prepped a new fleet of rental Jeeps without Granddad's supervision. With so many details, she feared overlooking something. It was a labor-intensive and time-consuming process, yet one that would pay off when the vehicles went to auction at the end of the season.

Standing by the bathroom sink, she grabbed her face wash and squeezed a small puddle of the creamy cleanser onto her fingertips. It was that attention to detail that kept customers coming back to Granddad's place year after year. Details Ross Chapman would never understand.

Who did he think he was, barging into her shop, threatening Adventures in Pink? The man made her angry enough to spit fire. The only good part of his visit was the look on Trent's face when he realized they weren't alone.

Fear tapped at the edge of Blakely's mind as she hovered over the marble vanity, scrubbing her face. Why did Trent have to show up now, after all these years? How would she explain things to Austin? He'd always been curious about his father, especially once he started school. Would he be mad at her? At Trent?

She pressed a hot-water-soaked washcloth against her cheeks and forehead. Trent must think her the same girl who'd once fallen for his boy-next-door routine. Accusing her of keeping Austin a secret in the next.

She tossed the rag into the sink and grabbed a soft white towel from the bar on the wall. *I don't want you to think I expect anything from you, Trent. Just know that I'd never keep this child, your child, from knowing his or her father.*

How she'd agonized over that dumb letter.

"Handwritten letters flow from your heart," Gran maintained, presenting Blakely with personalized stationery on every birthday, instilling a long-held appreciation for the dying art.

Well, that was one letter she wished she hadn't written. She never imagined Trent would wait ten years to take her up on her offer.

Slipping the towel back into place, Blakely glimpsed something in the mirror that she thought she'd buried long ago. Yet there it was, hidden behind steely determination and hundreds of freckles.

The sting of Trent's betrayal.

She took a deep breath and shook off the self-pity, vowing not to allow Trent or Ross to rob her of an enjoyable evening with her son.

In the kitchen, Blakely stared into the freezer, discounting chicken and pork chops before spotting a bag of frozen meatballs. She checked the pantry, giving herself a mental high five when she found both spaghetti sauce and noodles.

"Can't get much easier than that." Unless you counted cereal as a meal. And to her knowledge, Austin was the only one in the house who did.

She put a pot of water on to boil, then emptied the meatballs into a nonstick skillet. She nudged them around the pan as they sizzled.

Time had been kind to Trent. He'd always been ruggedly handsome, but now he was downright gorgeous.

Blakely froze, her spatula in midair. She'd lost her mind.

"You're just tired," she mumbled, returning her attention to the stove.

Not to mention lonely.

"Grrr." She transferred the contents of the skillet to a saucepan and dumped in the jar of tomato sauce.

"Maybe you could stay for dinner." Somewhere outside the window, Austin schemed with one of his friends. Luckily, spaghetti meant plenty to go around, so she wouldn't have to worry about seeing that disappointed frown of his.

A few moments later the front door flew open.

"Mom?" He rushed into the kitchen. "Can I invite a friend for dinner?"

"Sure. Who is it?"

"Trent."

Chapter Four

Trent's apprehension over Austin's dinner request paled in comparison to the look of horror on Blakely's face when she emerged from the kitchen. Pausing at the back of the sofa, she dug her fingers into the soft beige fabric until her knuckles were white.

He knew he should feel sorry for her, but sympathy was mitigated by his desire to spend time with his son. A son Blakely never told him about.

Austin seemed oblivious to the tension, though. "Mom, look what Trent taught me." In one quick movement, he gave his basketball a spin and uprighted it on his index finger, just like Trent had taught him. His brown eyes sparkled as he watched the rotating orb.

"Hey, you mastered it." A smiling, and seemingly more relaxed, Blakely dashed for a bookshelf. "We need a picture of this."

"Mom. You don't have to take a picture of everything."

Camera in hand, she paused. "Son, you know me better than that. Of course, I do."

Trent's gaze traversed the combined living and dining area. Nearly every surface, both vertical and horizontal, was adorned with family photos.

He had two. One of him as an infant with his mom and dad, and one of him and his mom, not long before she died.

He urged Austin forward. "Don't give your mom such a hard time."

Blakely held the digital camera in front of her and stared at the screen. "Ready?"

Austin gave the ball another spin and smiled.

After a brilliant flash, she checked the shot. "That'll make the scrapbook."

"The kid's got a persistent streak." Trent patted Austin on the back. "He worked at it all afternoon until he got it right."

Blakely's smile faltered. "You…spent the afternoon together?"

"Uh-huh." Austin shrugged. "I figured you wouldn't mind since you and Trent are friends." He set the ball beside the front door. "I can't wait to show Zach."

Trent and Blakely friends? At this point, that was stretching it. Though he could certainly hope.

"So you and Trent were playing basketball?" She shoved the camera back into its case, her wary gaze darting between father and son.

"At the park. He's really good."

"What are you talking about?" Trent poked a thumb in Austin's direction. "This turkey ran circles around me."

Ellie Mae sashayed into the room, stopping between Austin and Trent.

"There she is." He rubbed the dog's floppy ears. Just a big old bundle of love, that's what she was. "You're a good girl. Yes."

"Why, hello, Trent." Rose strolled into the room with Jethro tucked under her arm.

The little Yorkie barked once, stopping when Rose stroked his furry chin.

"Good evening, Mrs. D. And you, too, Jethro."

"This makes twice in one day," said Rose.

"Twice?" Accusation laced Blakely's tone. Seemed she'd been left in the dark on lots of things today.

"Yes, dear." Rose settled into one of two red swivel rockers and crossed her feet. "We ran into each other this morning, and Trent was kind enough to help me with my groceries."

Blakely regarded him but didn't say a word. He could only wonder what was going through that pretty head of hers.

"Well now, don't everybody stand around. Sit down, sit down." Rose waved a hand through the air, gesturing to the sofa and loveseat.

Trent snagged the loveseat in front of the window. "This place looks great, Mrs. D." Gone were the white walls and pink and blue furniture. Shades of gold and orange now warmed the space.

This house had been his haven that summer. Where he'd first experienced the true meaning of family. Though it didn't look anything like he remembered, an enormous amount of love still abounded in these four walls.

"Doesn't it, though?" Rose rocked gently back and forth. "After Bill died, Blakely said I needed a splash of color. I was a little leery at first, but she did a great job. I just love how cozy everything feels."

"She always did have an eye for color." His gaze drifted to the anxious strawberry blonde behind the couch. "But, then, one would expect that from an artist."

Her cheeks reddened. Just the reaction he was hoping for.

"Mom said Trent could stay for dinner." Austin flopped onto the sofa.

"Oh!" Blakely jumped and turned for the kitchen. "I almost forgot about dinner."

Trent excused himself and followed her, eager to find some way to ease the tension between them.

He found her frantically wiping the stove top when he entered. "Anything I can do to help?"

Halting midwipe, she hesitated before finally turning

around. "Um…" Eyes wide, she bit her bottom lip. Something he found sweet and…surprisingly irresistible.

He moved closer, intrigued as her gaze roamed his face, stopping at the scar on his forehead. Did she remember how it got there? That instead of holding that branch on their way up to Chief Ouray Mine, she'd let go. And five stitches later, she vowed to make him cookies twice a week until the end of August.

She looked away. "Actually, it's Austin's job to set the table."

Unwilling to let the moment go, he stepped closer, eliminating what little space remained between them.

"He's a great kid, Blakely. You've done a fantastic job."

She glanced up at him, her eyes glistening with unshed tears. "Thanks."

Blakely closed Austin's bedroom window and waited for him to finish brushing his teeth. Despite the recent warming trend, overnight temperatures still tumbled into the low forties. She wasn't about to risk him catching a cold.

Picking up the red hoodie from the floor, she savored the scent of little boy before hanging it in Austin's closet. What would she ever do without him? He was her world. What if Trent tried to take him away?

Austin appeared then. Wearing only pajama bottoms, he scooted under the green camouflage comforter, leaving room for Blakely to sit beside him. "We should take Trent Jeeping sometime."

Blakely feigned interest. She was sick of hearing about Trent, though, she supposed, she'd better get used to it. "What makes you think he'd be interested in tagging along with us?"

"He said so."

"Oh, he did, did he?" She straightened a stack of books on his headboard. What else might Trent instigate?

"Yeah. He said he likes going over the passes and stuff, but he's too chicken to drive."

She laughed. "*Chicken?* Was that your word or his?"

"His. I bet he'd like that place we found last summer. You know, the one off the old road to Imogene. Where we found the mine."

"Hey, short man, what have I told you about those mines? All kinds of danger can lurk in those things."

"I know. But they're so cool."

She ruffled his soft curls and kissed his cheek, thankful he still let her. "You need to get to sleep. It's late, and we've got church in the morning." Clicking off the lamp on his night-stand, she adjusted his covers one last time. "Sleep tight."

"Mom?"

"Yes." She waited at the foot of his bed.

"So, can we take Trent?"

"We'll see." It wasn't like her to be so noncommittal, especially where her son was concerned. But Trent's sudden appearance made it impossible to think straight.

Descending the stairs, she wondered how she'd even begin to tell Austin about his father. And prayed Trent wouldn't do so without discussing the matter with her first. When the time came, she'd make sure they told him together.

Downstairs, Gran sat in her rocker, knitting, while a rerun played on the television. Jethro snuggled beside her, and Ellie Mae was passed out at the front door. Probably waiting for Trent to return. You'd think the guy had bacon in his pockets the way she behaved.

"If you need me, I'm going to be taking a bath."

"Okay, dear."

Blakely retrieved her romance novel from the coffee table. She must enjoy torturing herself. Why else would she keep buying these love stories?

"You handled yourself very well tonight." Her grandmother twisted the needles and yarn.

"It sure didn't feel that way."

Gran peered over the top of her reading glasses. "You always knew this day might come."

"Yes, but I always thought I'd have time to prepare." She swiped at her dirty jeans. "And that I'd be better dressed." Which wasn't fair when Trent always seemed to look breathtakingly handsome.

Gran chuckled. "Well, I think we ought to give the young doctor a chance to prove himself."

"What?" Blakely lowered her voice to a whisper and dropped into the chair beside her grandmother. "How can you say that? After what he did to me?"

"This isn't just about you, dear." Gran leaned closer, laying a hand on Blakely's arm. "Yes, Trent made some bad choices. But you know as well as I do that we serve a God of second chances. Don't be so quick to judge." She winked. "You might miss a blessing."

Blakely shot to her feet. How dare Gran take Trent's side. "Austin *is* my blessing. And I never missed a thing."

Chapter Five

Blakely paced the empty Sunday School room. Out of the handful of churches in Ouray, what were the odds that Trent would show up at Restoration Fellowship? Now she faced the less-than-desirable prospect of sitting with him during worship.

"What are you doing in there?"

She turned to the voice coming from across the hall. Taryn Purcell, Ouray's best mountain guide, stared over the Dutch door that led to the church nursery.

"Just a little tidying up." As if to prove her point, she snatched a bulletin from a metal folding chair and tossed it into the trash.

Her friend lifted a brow. "Since when do you and four grayhaired ladies make a mess?"

Blakely frowned, surveying the tiny room. Even the chalkboard remained pristine.

"I guess I've got a lot on my mind." Piano music drifted from the sanctuary as she flipped off the light and crossed to the brightly colored children's area. *Vrooms* and crashing sounds echoed from the corner. Blakely smiled at two little boys playing cars. That had always been Austin's favorite, too.

"Must be an awful lot, then. It's not like you to lag behind."

Taryn stooped to pick up the Flint's two-year-old daughter clinging to her leg. "So what gives, Blakes?"

Her friend knew her too well.

The mural of Jesus and the little children on the opposite wall brightened what had once been a dingy, lifeless room. Hard to believe Austin was four when she painted that. Where had the time gone?

Her attention shifted back to Taryn. "More than I care to go into right now."

"All right, then. How about after our practice session? Think you can squeeze in some extra girl time?"

Blakely caressed the soft golden curls of the toddler in Taryn's arms. "I was hoping you might be available." Her secrets were safe with Taryn. Outside of Gran, she was the only one who knew the story of Austin's father. And she understood better than anyone else ever could. No doubt she'd also have a thing or two to say about Ross Chapman.

"You know I'm always here for you, Blakes. I'll even bring chocolate." Taryn's smile glinted in her aquamarine eyes.

"You're on, my friend."

Notes of "Blessed Be Your Name" filtered down the hall.

"I guess I'd better get in there before Austin gets worried."

"Yes, you should. And try to contain your excitement, would you?"

Anxiety knotted her stomach by the time she moved down the aisle. Thank goodness everyone was standing, making her late arrival less noticeable. Gran, Austin and Trent lined the pew on the third row, so she slipped in beside Gran and joined in the chorus.

When she stole a glimpse of her son, though, Blakely felt as though she were careening off of Imogene Pass.

Austin and Trent looked so much alike, it was like a six-inch time warp. A younger and older version of the same person. When people saw the two of them together, the rumor mill was bound to start churning, hard and fast. How long would she have before Austin started asking questions?

Her palms grew sweaty. She squeezed her eyes shut. *Lord, please make this go away. Make* him *go away.*

After the service, Trent followed them outside. Puffy white clouds meandered across the sky, but storms often lurked on the other side of the mountain.

"Mom, can Trent eat lunch with us?" The eagerness in her son's tone was hard to miss.

Trent touched the boy's shoulder. "Hold on there, Austin. I imposed on you guys last night. It's my turn to do the asking."

While Blakely cringed, Austin waited expectantly.

"I was thinking about heading over to Ridgway to grab some lunch at the True Grit Café. I'd be honored if you guys would join me."

"All right!" Austin turned to her, looking as though he might wiggle right out of his tanned skin. "You love their fish tacos."

"Yes, I do. However, Miss Taryn and I have plans this afternoon."

Gran waved to a fellow church member. "I thought that wasn't until three, dear."

"That's plenty of time, Mom. Come on. Please?"

The thought of having another family meal with Trent was about as appealing as a box of rocks. But that cherubic face pleading up at her made it impossible to say no.

Defeated, she let go a sigh. "Oh, all right. But we're not going to make this a habit." Though the words were directed at Austin, she glared at Trent.

"Great. My truck's parked right over there." He pointed to a white four-door pickup. "That is, if you don't mind me driving?"

Before she could respond, Austin ran ahead.

"You all have fun." Gran tucked today's bulletin inside her Bible.

"What?" Blakely's voice drifted up a notch. She quickly tempered it. "You mean you're not coming?"

"It's the third Sunday of the month, dear. Florence and I are doing brunch at Bon Ton." Her all-too-coy grandmother turned to leave, then paused and smiled. "However, you're certainly welcome to bring me a piece of the Grit's wonderful pie."

Trent couldn't help noticing the way Blakely hugged the passenger door of his pickup on the drive to Ridgway. Her ponytail was gone today, allowing waves of strawberry-blond curls to spill over her shoulders, free and easy. Now if only she'd loosen up.

Good thing they had Austin to keep things lively.

"Trent, did you know they made the movie *True Grit* here?" Austin poked his head between the front seats as Trent pulled into a parking space near the park. "The hanging scene was right over there."

"I don't believe it." He put the vehicle in Park.

"Really. It's true. Right, Mom?"

"Absolutely right." She opened her door, apparently eager to escape. Like being in these close quarters, having to endure the sweet fragrance of her shampoo, wasn't driving him crazy.

"That's why *True Grit*'s called True Grit." Austin hopped from the backseat, gravel crunching when his feet hit the ground.

"You ever see that movie?"

"Lots of times. John Wayne is cool."

Trent stepped down, his thumbs dangling from his belt loops. "I'd have to agree with you there, Pilgrim." A lame impersonation of The Duke, but Austin laughed anyway.

Though the soft giggle that filtered through the cab was what really got his attention. He'd missed that laugh. Hoped to hear more of it. Even if it meant pulling out his Elvis impersonation.

Across the street, he held the door open as Blakely followed Austin inside the restaurant.

The True Grit Café, a longtime favorite of locals and tourists alike, hummed with energy, not to mention the aromas of Tex-Mex and comfort food that made his stomach growl.

A ponytailed brunette scurried from behind the *L*-shaped bar and across the wood floor. "Table for three?"

He nodded.

The young woman grabbed a stack of menus and led them past the stone fireplace to a booth at the back of the restaurant.

Blakely slid in beside Austin as the waitress handed out menus and took their drink orders.

"Look." Trent pointed to a picture of a young John Wayne hanging on the wall next to them. "We get to eat with The Duke."

Never mind that every other patron did, too. Movie memorabilia lined the walls of the restaurant. And though actor Dennis Weaver had been Ridgway's most famous citizen, John Wayne still reigned as king at the Grit.

Cheek resting on his fist, Austin opened his menu. "You're so weird."

Trent's mouth fell open. His first slam. Oh, no.

Opposite him, Blakely struggled to contain her laughter. "Welcome to the wonderful world of—" She stopped, leaving off the proverbial "parenthood." "I mean, welcome to my—"

World, he was tempted to add.

Finally, she gestured to their son. "See what I have to put up with?"

He shouldn't get enjoyment from watching her squirm, but he couldn't help it. She looked so darn cute in pink.

Now she hid behind her menu.

Trent tried to focus on his own. "What are you getting, Austin?"

"I can't decide. Either tacos or a hamburger. They have the *best* hamburgers."

"That we do, young man." The waitress deposited their drinks, tucked the small tray under her arm and withdrew a pad from the pocket of her black apron. "So what would you like to order?"

After a few moments of indecision, Austin opted for the burger. Trent joined him, while Blakely ordered the fish tacos.

"Hey, Trent." Austin swirled a straw through his Sprite, watching the tiny bubbles on the sides of the glass. "Did you know Adventures in Pink is the best tour company in Ouray?"

"So I hear." He emptied a packet of sugar into his iced tea, glancing Blakely's way. "By the way, when did The Jeep Company become Adventures in Pink?"

"About seven years ago." She peeled the plastic covering from her straw and poked it into her glass of water. "Granddad wanted something to set us apart. We toyed with the idea of red, but that was too generic." She took a sip. "Pink started as a joke. But the more we thought about it, the more we liked it. Especially once we came up with the name Adventures in Pink."

"And I see you're doing more than Jeep tours."

"Hence the adventure part." She unrolled the napkin from around her silverware and laid it across her lap. "By teaming up with businesses in Telluride and Ridgway, we now offer river rafting, fly-fishing, even hot air balloon rides."

"Sounds like strategic marketing."

"That was our goal. Even if folks don't remember our name, all they have to do is mention the pink Jeeps."

"Austin, how do you feel about the pink theme?" Trent swigged his tea.

"It's pretty cool. I still think they should have flames, though."

A sudden burst of laughter had him choking and coughing. "You may be on to something, buddy." His voice cracked as another cough escaped.

"You okay?"

Was that a note of concern in Blakely's query?

"Raise your arm over your head," said Austin.

Trent swiped a napkin across his mouth, blew out a slow breath and took another drink. "I'm okay." He cleared his throat one more time. "But I'd have to agree with Austin. I think flames might be just the right touch."

She lifted a brow. "Uh…no."

"Here we are." The waitress placed each order in front of its owner.

"Wow." Trent stared at the half-pound buffalo burger on his plate. "Now that's what I call a burger."

"Wait till you taste it." Austin chomped on a French fry.

"Anything else I can get you folks?"

"No, I think we're good." With the waitress gone, Trent glanced at Austin then Blakely. "Shall we pray?"

Blakely grabbed Austin's hand. Then, as if it were the most natural thing in the world, Austin stretched his other hand across the table toward Trent.

The simplest of gestures, yet one that meant so much.

He clasped Austin's hand, then offered Blakely his other.

The softness of her touch sent a wave of awareness through him. And, for a split second, it was as though they were a family.

Dreams he'd tucked away long ago drifted to the surface. Could he still have the one thing that had eluded him all his life?

Maybe…if he wasn't going back to Albuquerque at the end of the summer.

Unfortunately, he'd made commitments that demanded just that.

Many are the plans in a man's heart, but it's the Lord's purpose that prevails.

The verse played across his mind as he blessed their meal. God had a plan. He knew about Austin long before Trent did.

It was Trent's job to trust God to work things out according to that plan.

Attacking the massive buffalo burger, Trent savored the perfectly seasoned meat.

Austin swallowed his first bite of the burger. Licked ketchup from his fingers. "Mom, did you know Trent had a horse?"

"No, I didn't." She dared to meet the man's gaze. "I don't imagine Vivian is letting you keep that at the inn."

"No." He smiled. "She's part of an equine therapy program in Albuquerque."

"Trent said he'd take me riding sometime."

He cut a quick look at Austin. "*If* it's all right with your mom."

Now they both stared at Blakely as another waitress skirted past carrying a large food-laden tray.

"That'd be fine." She gripped the first of her two fish tacos. "As long as you wear a helmet."

"A helmet?" Trent and Austin blurted at the same time.

"Mom, I'd look like a dweeb."

Trent pointed to the photos on the wall. "John Wayne never wore a helmet."

"Yes, but I wasn't John Wayne's mother."

Multiple conversations and the clanking of silverware and dishes filled the subsequent silence.

"I'll think about it," Blakely finally said, brightening Austin's mood.

He straightened, a smile lighting his face. "It's not as dangerous as the fire hose water fights."

"I love the fire hose fights." Trent set his burger down, recalling the only Independence Day he'd ever spent in Ouray but would always be remembered as the best. "Next to the fireworks, that's the best part of the Fourth of July."

Austin leaned his arms on the table. "I know. And Mom's gonna be in 'em again this year."

His gaze shifted to Blakely. "You mean you're *in* the fire hose fights?"

Her chewing slowed. She nodded.

"Yeah. She did it last year. Only her team lost," Austin filled in for her.

"We're planning on a different outcome this year." She reached for her water. "Taryn and I have a new strategy."

"Which is...?" Trent lifted a brow in anticipation.

"Pffft. Like I'd tell." And there it was. The old playful Blakely he'd fallen in love with. Her guard was down, and she was enjoying the banter.

"You shoulda seen it, Trent. Mom had like this giant black bruise on her leg."

"Sounds kind of dangerous." He turned a concerned eye her way.

"Not really."

"Yeah. She's a tough cookie." Austin smiled up at her.

She winked. "That's what Granddad used to say."

Austin's attention shifted back to Trent. "My mom does ice climbing, too. *And* she's an artist."

Trent didn't need Austin to tell him how wonderful his mother was. He knew firsthand. And, if he had his way, he wouldn't mind getting to know Blakely all over again. But that would require forgiveness. Something she wasn't likely to offer him anytime soon.

Heat rushed to Blakely's cheeks until she was, no doubt, as red as Trent's button-down shirt. It didn't take a genius to figure out what her son was up to. The kid was trying to fix her up with Trent. Never had she seen him so enamored with someone.

Staring at her second taco, she all but lost her appetite. The little guy didn't have a clue. All he knew was that he liked Trent. Enough that he wanted to play matchmaker for his mother.

"Fancy running into you folks again."

Blakely jerked her head up to find Ross Chapman standing next to them. Beside him, his daughter, Nicole, struck a pose in her hip-hugging jeans and too-tight T-shirt.

Blakely's first taco morphed into a lead weight in her stomach.

"Ross." She forced herself to blink. "Nicole."

Trent stood. "Mr. Chapman. Nice to see you again."

"No need to be formal. Call me Ross." He swiveled toward the young woman. "I'd like you to meet my daughter, Nicole."

Slightly younger than Blakely's twenty-nine years, Nicole was her daddy's pride and joy. And forever trolling for a husband. Preferably one with big biceps and an even bigger wallet.

Blakely stole a glance at Trent. Hmm…a doctor would fit that bill just fine. And Trent certainly had the biceps. The man obviously never missed a workout.

The platinum blonde struck a flirtatious pose and held a perfectly manicured hand in Trent's direction. "I hear you're a doctor."

Bingo!

"That's correct." Trent barely shook her hand. Then again, it was kind of like shaking hands with a wet noodle.

Nicole's gaze lingered a little longer than necessary— stirring emotions Blakely refused to own up to—before turning her heavily made up face Blakely's way. "Blakely. Austin. Good to see y'all." If that Texas twang got any thicker it would drip like honey.

"You, too." Blakely nudged her son. "Austin, can you say hi?"

"Hi." He waved.

Nicole waved back, watching him a moment before her green eyes returned to Trent.

"I swear, Blakely, that boy of yours gets bigger every time I see him." Though Ross's words were polite enough, she'd had enough dealings with him to realize they weren't sincere.

"He's at that age where they change so quickly. Better make sure you enjoy every moment."

And there went the zinger. Ross's not-so-subtle hint that she should sell Adventures in Pink so she could spend more time with her son.

"Oh, don't you worry about that." Blakely draped an arm around her son. "Austin's my right-hand man."

Nicole's gaze flitted from Austin to Trent and back again, shifting Blakely's panic into full throttle. Nicole might act the part of a dumb blonde; however, she was anything but. More like shrewd and discerning. And definitely not one to dismiss the similarities between Austin and Trent without digging further.

"As it should be." Ross placed a hand on the small of his daughter's back and urged her away. "You folks enjoy your lunch."

Too late. He'd already ruined it.

Trent settled back into the booth. "That was…awkward."

"Trust me. It could have been worse." Blakely moved her shaky hands to her lap. If the Chapmans had the slightest inkling that Trent was Austin's father, they'd find some way to use it against her.

Trent lowered his head a notch. "You okay?"

Far from it. But she couldn't let on in front of Austin. "Fine."

"You've barely touched your other taco."

"I think I ate the first one too fast." She grazed a hand over her stomach. "I'll take it home and have it later."

"Excuse me, please." Austin wiggled next to her.

"Too many sodas?" She stood to let him out.

"Yes, ma'am."

In Austin's absence, Trent tucked his paper napkin beside his empty plate. "There's a lot we need to talk about."

If it involved custody of Austin, she wanted no part of it.

Her shoulders slumped. "I suppose. But not while Austin's around."

"Agreed."

She faced him, mustering enough courage to ask the question that had plagued her most. "Trent, are you going to try to take Austin away from me?"

"I don't think I can answer that right now. I'm still trying to absorb the fact that he's my son."

His answer was fair enough. Still, that question would be her constant companion.

"Can I ask you a favor?"

"Anything."

"Please don't tell him who you are without me."

"Blakely, I wouldn't...." He raked a hand through his hair before clasping the other atop the table. "There's so much I want to know about him."

She jiggled the ice in her now-empty glass. "Like what?"

"Like...his middle name?"

"Blake."

"After your father." His voice was endearingly gentle.

She nodded.

"I like it. Is he always so easygoing?"

"For the most part."

"When's his birthday?"

"Who's birthday?"

Trent's uneasy expression mirrored her own. Was that all Austin had heard?

"Yours, of course." Emotions collided as she scooted over to let him sit down. The day Austin was born was the happiest of Blakely's life. It was also the saddest.

"June first," Austin announced with pride.

"That's coming up pretty quick, isn't it?" Trent seemed to relax once again.

"Yeah. Hey, maybe you could come to my birthday."

Blakely glanced from Trent to the Chapmans.

This day just kept getting better and better.

Chapter Six

The sun seemed brighter as Trent strode across the courtyard of the San Juan Inn that afternoon.

If he'd had any idea what treasures Ouray had in store for him, he would have found his way back years ago. His marriage had been over long before Lauren's boyfriend wrapped his fancy sports car around that light pole. It seemed the closer Trent grew to the Lord, the greater the distance between him and his wife. In the end, the accident merely meant Trent would never have to sign the divorce papers he'd been avoiding for months.

Maybe you could come to my birthday.

The innocent words of a child—his child—soothed the tattered edges of his heart. The only thing sweeter would be to hear someone call him "Dad."

He smiled and unlocked the door to his room. Soon.

A million questions plagued his brain. Everything and nothing all at once. The minutia. Not only of Austin, but Blakely. Did she still want to be an artist? Why did Ross Chapman make her so nervous? Was that spot behind her ear still ticklish?

Whoa. Wrong train of thought. Stuff like that was what got them to this point in the first place.

He tossed his keys on the nightstand and fished the vibrating cell phone out of his pocket. A stiff dose of reality hit him when he glanced at the screen.

"Hey, Scott."

"Good news, buddy." His friend sounded excited enough for the both of them. "The building passed inspection. We close June fifteenth."

Trent dropped onto the bed. "That soon, huh? Tha—that's great."

"Can you believe it? Everything we've talked about since medical school is finally coming to fruition."

Trent rubbed the back of his neck. Opening a small private practice was his dream. But he also dreamed of having a family. Or had, until Lauren dropped the bomb that she didn't want children. So he tucked away those desires and concentrated on his career.

"Our own practice," Scott continued. "Do you know what this means?"

That he'd be in Albuquerque while his son was in Ouray. "What?"

"No more thirty-six-hour E.R. shifts."

"Yep." That part he liked. Leaving Austin? Not so much.

But he'd made a commitment to Scott. They'd planned and scouted locations for months. Pooled their resources. If he backed out, the dream they worked so hard for would fall apart.

"Rebecca can't wait to start decorating. She's got me looking at paint swatches as we speak."

He could hear Scott's four-year-old daughter, Daisy, singing in the background. His friend had the whole package. A promising career, a wife, a beautiful little girl…

"What do you think, green or blue?"

He stared beyond the lace curtain, up the face of Twin Peaks. "I'm sure whatever Rebecca chooses will be great."

Ending the call, he lay back on the queen-size bed and stared up at the ceiling.

God, please help me. I know I messed up. On multiple lev-

els. But I don't want my son to grow up without knowing his father. Been there, done that. I don't want Austin to have those same questions and doubts.

He could spend summers with Austin. School breaks, perhaps long weekends. Albuquerque was only six hours away.

But it wouldn't be the same.

Unfortunately, it would have to do. He'd given his word.

And he never went back on his word.

Blakely kicked off her pointy-toe flats and shut the bedroom door behind her before ditching the rest of her church clothes for workout pants and a T-shirt. Today was the first time she and Taryn would get a chance to test their new strategy for the fire hose fights. Hopefully, the technique would work as well in execution as it did in theory.

Cinching the drawstring on her sweats, Blakely groaned. Near as she could tell, Austin still didn't suspect Trent was his father. Though he did think the man was the best thing since video games. And she had to admit, she enjoyed their time together, too. Watching Austin share what he considered her greatest assets.

She flopped back onto the full-size bed and stared at the silver faux-finished ceiling. For the shortest of moments today, they'd seemed like a real family.

Allowing her mind to linger on that life-changing summer, she pushed herself upright and went to her closet. She moved clothes out of the way, digging until she found a plain cardboard box. Her heart thudded as she set the box on the plum-colored comforter. After a long moment, she pulled opened the flaps.

She smiled as she set aside Austin's baby book, his first pair of hiking boots and the outfit he wore home from the hospital. Then she saw it. The small box buried at the bottom.

With a deep breath, she reached for it, her pulse racing. She laid it in the palm of her hand, carefully, as if it were a bomb that might detonate at any second. Finally, she lifted the hinged lid and stared at the set of artist brushes.

A card with white tulips, her favorite flower, lay on top. She opened it and read.

Dear Blakely. These aren't as romantic as diamonds or pearls, but the sentiment is still the same. I hope you'll think of me every time you use them, until we can be together again.
Love, Trent.

She returned the card to the box, allowing her fingertips to linger over the soft bristles. Knowing Trent had spent his hard-earned money—money that was supposed to go toward college—warmed her heart, the same way it had the day he'd given them to her.

She'd used them once.

Her gaze fell back to the larger box. Tucked against one side was a small, square canvas. She reached for it, then hesitated. With a bolstering breath, she latched on to the oil painting and turned it around.

Root beer eyes smiled at her under deep brown curls. She'd painted the picture of Trent from memory after he left for Albuquerque that dreadful September day. Each brushstroke seemed to help her deal with the heartache of saying goodbye.

She tossed the brushes and the canvas back inside the box. What if things had been different? What if Trent had married her? Would every day be as delightful as today?

Tears pooled in her eyes. She blinked, and they spilled down her cheeks. Using her sleeves, she dabbed them away. No more tears. Hadn't that been her promise all those years ago?

No one could change their past. She could only look toward the future. No matter how unsteady it seemed.

* * *

By the time Blakely met Taryn at Rotary Park, her mood was on the upswing. All winter long they had strategized about how they needed to work as a unit. Today, those ideas proved successful. Now they watched, satisfied with their trial run, as the fire hose was recoiled onto the truck.

"I don't know about you, but I'm ready for that chocolate I promised." Taryn retrieved two bottles of water and two one-pound bags of M&M's from the front seat of her silver Jeep Rubicon. "I couldn't decide what kind of mood I'd be in, so I brought both plain and peanut."

Blakely followed her to a nearby picnic table as the fire engine rumbled away. "I'm happy with either one."

"Good." Her friend tore open the yellow bag. "Right now, I'm feeling a little nutty."

Blakely accepted a handful of the colorful candies. "Probably because you are."

"Takes one to know one." Popping a yellow and green into her mouth, Taryn sat down opposite her. "So, what's up?"

May as well start at the beginning. "Ross Chapman offered to buy Adventures in Pink."

"What? Why?"

The harmonious blend of milk chocolate and peanuts danced on Blakely's tongue, dulled only by the topic of conversation. "Who knows? I'm guessing he sees us as a threat. Probably thought I'd be a pushover. Get this—" she leaned her folded arms on the table "—he tried to tell me it was my duty to take care of my family, not run a business."

"Gee, as I recall, your grandfather did both of those things."

"Yes, but he was a man."

Taryn ripped open the brown bag. "Chauvinist." Poured a handful. "So what did you tell him?"

"No, of course. But that hasn't stopped him. Every time I turn around he's slinking up on me. At the shop. Even at lunch today." The more she talked about it, the more agitated she got.

She swiped sweaty palms down the jersey cotton of her workout pants. "He even threatened to use my accident against me."

"How?"

She deepened her voice. "'Word travels fast. Hope it doesn't hurt your business.'"

"Chapman is such a sleazeball." Taryn peeled off her do-rag, her short golden-brown hair falling around her face. "He knows Mountain View Tours can't compete with Adventures in Pink. You just stand your ground, Blakes, because there's not a business owner in town who wouldn't stand with you."

Her friend's encouragement made her smile. "Thanks."

"Now, would you like to tell me what else has you so wound up?"

Letting go a sigh, Blakely grabbed another handful of chocolate for strength. "Austin's father is back in town."

Taryn's aquamarine eyes grew wide. Her mouth fell open, but she closed it without saying a word.

"This is a first. I've actually rendered you speechless."

"Wow. You mean he just showed up?"

"Pretty much." Eyeing the dark clouds inching over Twin Peaks, she explained how things had transpired.

"He said you never told him about Austin?"

"Yep."

"But you did, didn't you?"

"Yes." She dropped a red-coated morsel in her mouth. "His then-girlfriend assured me he received my letter."

"Double wow." Concentrating on nothing in particular, Taryn opened her bottle and took a drink. "What does your grandmother have to say about all of this?"

"She told me not to cast judgment. That I should give him a chance to prove himself."

Pausing, her friend reached for more chocolate. "You're gonna hate me for this, but she's got a point."

"Pardon me?" A sudden gust of frigid air made Blakely wish she'd brought a jacket.

"I may be playing devil's advocate, but what if he didn't know?"

"Oh, he knew all right."

"Are you certain?"

"Whose side are you on?"

Taryn grabbed her hand. "Yours. Always. But let's think about this. He lost his wife and baby."

"Is this supposed to make me feel better?"

Obviously sensing Blakely's desire to pull away, her grip tightened. "Oh, shush and listen to me. Eleven years is a long time. People change. You know better than anyone that I'm not the same person I was eleven years ago."

Blakely recalled the spoiled high-schooler who couldn't wait to trade her hiking boots for stilettos and big city lights. "No, you're not."

"And you were the first person to befriend me when I came back to Ouray."

"Yeah, I've always been a sucker for that lost puppy look." One of the things that had initially drawn her to Trent. Not that he wasn't strong and independent. He'd just looked so forlorn.

"Whatever." Rolling her eyes, Taryn reached for her water bottle. "You know good and well you were the first person willing to give me a second chance." She uncapped the plastic bottle, a smug grin firmly in place. "And you ended up with the best friend anyone could ask for."

"Ha!" Listening to the sound of slowing traffic on asphalt, she satisfied her own thirst. "So what am I supposed to do? Welcome Trent with open arms and say, 'Here's your son'?"

"I didn't say don't be cautious."

Though no one else was around, she lowered her voice. "What would you do if your baby's father showed up?"

"I've been sitting here asking myself the same question."

"And?"

"Well, if the old Taryn were still around, she might hire a hit man." They both chuckled. "And while I still might be tempted…" Her expression turned serious. "I honestly don't know how I'd react. But, then, I didn't keep my baby."

The melancholy that clouded her features had Blakely reaching for her. "And you did the right thing."

"I know. I just meant the circumstances would be different. Have you told Austin yet?"

Blakely shook her head. "But I won't be able to hold out for long. They look too much alike. Tongues are bound to start wagging."

"Sweetie, the best advice I can give you is to commit this to prayer. Assuming you haven't already."

"Well…." Truth was, she'd spent more time trying to figure out how to fix things. "Sort of."

"Blakes, asking God to make it go away does not count."

Drat!

"Remember, there are no coincidences. If Trent's here, God has a reason for it."

Taryn emptied the yellow bag into her hand. "Wow. We made quick work of that."

"Yeah." Blakely rubbed her stomach. "And I have a feeling I'm going to be paying for it the rest of the night."

Thunder rumbled in the distance.

"Uh-oh." Taryn turned to investigate the cloud-filled sky behind her. "Looks like things could get nasty."

"Yeah, I need to make sure Austin is home."

They stood and tossed their trash on the way to their respective Jeeps.

"Thanks for letting me vent." She hugged her friend.

"Anytime, girlfriend. Anytime. After all, there aren't many people around here who'd understand what we've been through."

That common ground of being young, unwed mothers had forged a strong bond between her and Taryn. Not even Taryn's family knew she'd been pregnant, let alone given her baby up for adoption.

She squeezed her friend tighter. God had brought them together. Each finding safe haven in the other. One where secrets were shared, never to be repeated. A friendship bound by understanding and a love for their children that was so strong, it gave them the courage to do things they never thought they could.

Which was a good thing. Because right now, Blakely needed more courage than she ever imagined.

Chapter Seven

Three days with no signs of Trent or Ross. Blakely's luck must be changing. At least in some respects.

Surrounded by the familiar smells of rubber and gasoline, she hunched over the engine of a tour vehicle while Dan pointed out the faulty water pump. "That thing's gonna be a bear to get to."

"Yeah, it'll take a while." He straightened, wiped his hands on a rag. "But then she should be good to go."

Taking a step back, she slid her hands into the back pockets of her faded jeans. "Well, better we get it taken care of now. Before the big holiday weekend."

Dan's gaze shifted behind her. "Hey there, Doc."

Blakely's heart dropped somewhere in the vicinity of her knees.

Doc? That could only mean one thing.

She eased around, the turkey sandwich she'd just eaten for lunch churning in her belly.

Clad in dark-wash jeans and a brown leather jacket, Trent looked like he'd just stepped from the pages of a magazine. "Don't let me interrupt."

"Nah, you're fine." Dan moseyed across the concrete floor and shook Trent's hand. "We're finished anyway."

"Finished. Yes." One-word sentences. Nothing like showing the guy what kind of affect he had on her.

"Good." He gave Blakely his full attention now. "I was wondering if you might have some time to talk."

Here it comes. The conversation she'd been dreading. The one where Trent told her he wanted her son.

Squaring her shoulders, she peered up at Dan. "Can you hold down the fort for a bit?"

"No problem, boss."

She whisked past Trent, determined to keep the upper hand. After all, she had nothing to be sorry for. She'd been truthful with him from the beginning. She was the one who'd devoted her life to Austin.

"There's a Jeep out back. I'll meet you there." She grabbed her jacket and keys from the office before joining Trent behind the building.

Blakely hurled herself into the driver's side, fastened her seatbelt and started the engine.

"Where are we going?"

She grabbed hold of the gear shift and eased off of the clutch. "Some place no one will overhear us."

Heading south on Main Street, she wound the switchbacks leading out of town before turning off near Box Cañon.

Trent grabbed hold of the dash as she swung onto Campbird Road, a move that had her laughing inside.

"I assume you want to discuss Austin." She barreled over the Uncompahgre Gorge, a premiere destination for ice climbers in the winter.

"Among other things."

Other things? What kind of other things?

Forests of aspen and pine lined the county road, and the air grew cooler as they climbed. Trent zipped his jacket but didn't say a word.

Fine by her. She wasn't in the mood for idle chitchat.

Soon the trees were replaced by a wall of rock on their

right and a wide canyon on the left. Not far from where she had her accident.

She wasn't about to repeat that mistake. Despite somewhat drier conditions, she eyed the rocky terrain above, looking for any sign of movement.

The engine groaned under the steep inclines so she shifted into four-wheel drive and continued on. The contrasting beauty of dense woods and barren rock formations spread around them. Snow clung to crevices. Trees perched precariously on miniscule outcroppings, whereas others had been swept away by avalanches.

Near the abandoned mining town of Sneffels, she turned onto another trail. Runoff tunneled under a heavy blanket of snow and the creek lay before them. Any other time she'd have used the bridge. But why not throw a little adventure Trent's way? Catch him off guard.

Without hesitating, she continued headlong through the steady current. Water splashed over the tires, and ice-cold droplets pelted them both.

He pointed to the bridge. "You know, they probably put that thing there for a reason."

"Yeah. For chickens."

He shook his head, apparently not as rattled as she thought he'd be. "And this from the woman who wants her son to wear a helmet horseback riding."

On the other side of the stream, she brought the Jeep to a halt and turned off the engine. Her insides felt like one giant pretzel.

"So are you going to charge me for this tour, or is this a freebie?" Trent laughed at his own joke, but she ignored his lame attempt to break the ice.

Undoing his seatbelt, he turned to face her. "Look, the main thing I want to know is why you didn't tell me about Austin. Did you feel like you couldn't, or were you trying to get back at me?"

Why did he insist on blaming her for this? "You're determined to play the victim, aren't you?"

"What?"

"Don't try to deny it. I know for a fact that you received my letter."

His brow puckered. "Letter? What letter?"

Tossing her seatbelt aside, she hopped out of the vehicle and stormed up the rocky slope.

Trent followed. "What letter, Blakely?"

"You remember. The one where I told you I was pregnant and that I didn't expect anything from you." She marched around a massive pine. "The one where I promised not to keep your child from you. Which, I assume, is why you're here now."

Trent struggled to keep up. "Blakely, I promise you, I never received any letter."

Pausing, she balled her fists in the pockets of her jacket and turned to face him. "Sorry. But she told me you did."

"Who told you?"

"Lauren." She sighed, the memory of that day seared in her mind's eye. "When I finally got up the courage to phone you, she answered. Even called me by name. She said you'd gotten my letter and was surprised you hadn't contacted me yet."

The color drained from Trent's face. He stumbled to a nearby boulder and dropped. "How can that be? I—I never knew about any of this." His gaze found hers again. "Why didn't you say something when I told you I was getting married?"

"Oh, so this is my fault now?"

"I didn't say that."

She scuffed the toe of her hiking boot across a dwindling mound of snow. "I would have sounded like a desperate fool, and that's not my style."

"So all these years you thought I turned my back on you."

"Because you did."

"No. I didn't." He pushed to his feet, his frustration evident as he began to pace. "Blakely, I— Please? Would you at least consider the possibility? What if I didn't receive your letter?" Those dark brown eyes pleaded with her to believe him.

Stay strong. Don't cave.

She studied the gathering clouds, then shrugged. "You made your choice. What difference would it have made anyway?"

"The difference was I loved you."

How long had she waited to hear those words? Now she doubted they were even true.

She turned for the Jeep, pausing at the door. "We can play what-ifs all day long, Trent, but the facts are still the same. You got two women pregnant that summer. That's not the kind of father I envisioned for my son."

Trent hadn't felt so befuddled since he was four years old and the social workers told him his mother had died.

Both he and Blakely maintained their silence on the drive back to town. What else was there to say? He certainly couldn't refute what she'd said. Though hearing her say the words was like a knife through the heart.

Still numb, he excused himself once they reached Adventures in Pink and began the trek back to his motel. He knew when to retreat.

He'd barely made it to the corner, though, when the weight of his actions made his legs feel like he was plodding through knee-deep mud. Dropping onto the metal bench outside of one of the gift shops, he rested his forearms on his thighs and stared up at the ominous gray sky.

Lord, what have I done?

The truth of Blakely's words ate at him like a stage-four cancer. His sin had affected so many lives. How could he ever begin to make up for the pain he'd caused?

"Whatever you're contemplating can't be good." Without waiting for an invitation, Dan settled beside him. Concern furrowed his brow. "You okay?"

"Not really." Trent continued to study the gathering gloominess overhead, feeling more than a little sorry for himself.

"My wife says I'm a pretty good listener." Dan stretched his long denim-clad legs in front of him, crossing them at the ankles. "Comes with the job description, I guess. Preacher, that is, not mechanic."

Trent had been more than a little surprised on Sunday to discover Dan was the pastor at Restoration Fellowship. And that Lisa, the receptionist at Adventures in Pink, was his wife.

Now he regarded the kindhearted man beside him. Back in Albuquerque, Trent's pastor had been his closest confidant. If Dan weren't so close to Blakely, he might consider the offer.

"Thanks, but I'm just being melodramatic."

"I'd say you're a pretty good actor, then." Dan folded his arms over his chest and leaned closer. "How long have you known he's your son?"

Trent's gaze flicked to Dan, his eyes widening in disbelief. "She told you?"

"Didn't have to. Between the physical resemblance and the way Blakely flinches whenever you're around, I drew my own conclusions."

Trent blew out a slow breath, the descending clouds obscuring the gray volcanic peaks of the Amphitheater. How many other people had the same suspicions? "I could be truthful and tell you I didn't know until that day up on the mountain, but you probably wouldn't believe me."

"Why do you say that?"

"Blakely swears I knew all along."

"But, you didn't?"

"No. If I had, wild horses couldn't have kept me away." Trent looked up and down the row of colorful historic storefronts, cautious of anyone who might care to listen in on their conversation. "Unfortunately, things are more complicated than simply finding out I have a son."

"I gathered as much. Blakely's not one to get her feathers

ruffled. But lately…" Dan hesitated. Drawing in his legs, he rested his palms against the seat and leaned forward. "Trent, for what it's worth, you don't strike me as the kind of guy who'd turn his back on a child. Or his mother, for that matter."

An eighteen-wheeler rumbled past, giving Trent time to consider Dan's comments.

When the diesel cleared, Dan continued, "I take it Austin doesn't know?"

Trent shook his head. "And if Blakely has her way, he never will."

"I have a hard time imagining that. She's expressed Austin's need for a male role model many times."

"Well, she definitely doesn't want me to be that role model. You know, Dan, I came to Ouray to take a break from my life in Albuquerque. God seemed to open doors every step of the way. Then I found out about Austin, and I felt like God had given me a second chance."

"You sound as though you're rethinking that stance."

Trent looked up at the shrouded mountaintops. *I lift up my eyes to the hills—where does my help come from?*

My help comes from the Lord.

Peace flooded his soul, eradicating the turmoil he'd let cloud his judgment. God would help him through this rocky patch as He had every other time life didn't go as Trent had hoped. But first he had to give God the reins.

A smile tugged at the corners of his mouth. "Not at all. But He is going to make me work for it."

"He has a habit of doing that." Dan sent him an understanding look along with a slap on the back. "But if you follow His lead, I guarantee it'll be worth it."

The sound of happy children interrupted the afternoon lull, and Dan shifted his attention to the opposite corner. "School's out." He scanned the darkening sky. "And, from the looks of things, just in time, too."

"You have kids?"

"One." Dan stood and pointed toward a trio of little girls. "See the girl with the dark ponytail?"

"Looks like Lisa."

Dan choked out a laugh. "Lucky for her."

Trent pushed to his feet, a sense of hope renewing his strength. "How old?"

"Six." Dan started toward the crosswalk. "Why don't you come meet her?"

"Trent!" Across the street Austin waved, and Trent's spirits soared.

Dan nudged him. "I had a feeling he'd be close by. Austin watches out for my Alyssa."

Pride swelled in Trent's chest. Austin was a good kid.

He had Blakely to thank for that.

"You know what, Dan? No matter how hard I have to work to make things right, it will *definitely* be worth the effort."

Chapter Eight

Blakely closed the spreadsheet on the computer screen, her office chair groaning as she slumped against the padded back. She'd never ripped into anyone the way she'd ripped into Trent. On the drive back to town, she couldn't even look at him. The expression on his face. So genuine. Raw. Like how she felt when she learned of her father's plane crash. Denial, hurt and anger all rolled into one excruciating emotion.

Could someone really fake that?

She stared at a collage of snapshots on the wall. Austin with his first bike. His first day of school. His first puppy, Ellie Mae. Years of memories. And Trent had missed every one of them.

I loved you.

Her eyes fell closed. She used to dream of hearing Trent say those words. Dream he'd come back for her and Austin.

But he didn't.

Because he didn't know.

"Everything okay in here?"

Blakely opened her eyes to see Lisa leaning against the open door. Forcing a smile she certainly didn't feel, she hoped to erase any trace of melancholy. "Of course. What would make you think otherwise?"

"School let out over ten minutes ago. You're usually out front waiting on Austin."

Blakely jumped to her feet, eyeing her watch. "Goodness. You're right." She pushed past Lisa. Since when had she become so predictable? "I guess I got so caught up in payroll that I lost track of time."

"Funny. You usually hate doing payroll."

Lisa was too observant.

Blakely continued around the counter, toward the front door. "I know. Weird, huh? Thanks for keeping me on task, Lisa."

The screen creaked open, and Blakely stepped onto the porch, hoping to rid herself of the funk that had plagued her all afternoon. She didn't want Austin to see her like this.

She zipped her jacket and folded her arms to ward against the chill that had invaded the air. It would rain soon. And from the looks of the steely clouds racing over Hayden's peak, they could be in for another stormy evening.

Across the street, a doe snacked on the neighbor's lawn. Given the impending weather, Blakely was surprised the animal hadn't run for cover. Perhaps things wouldn't be as bad as she thought. Goodness knows she had a habit of overthinking things.

She descended the concrete steps, turning her focus in the direction of Main Street. Austin was already at the corner, talking with Dan and Alyssa. Not a care in the world. Would you look at that megawatt smile?

His sweet disposition would go a long way toward improving her mood. Hard to believe her little man would be ten in less than a week. Definitely a cause for celebration. His party had been booked at the hot springs pool for more than a month, but she still had to give Taryn the details on his cake. Nothing but fudge marble would do.

Dan waved as he and Alyssa walked away, and Blakely's heart wrenched when she spotted the source of Austin's delight.

Even from half a block away, she could see the pain etched on Trent's handsome face. And regardless of their past, it was a handsome face.

Blakely, I promise you, I never received any letter.

Squeezing her arms tighter, she stared at the gathering clouds. Blinked away moisture.

God, could it really be true?

Mentally turning back the pages of time, she thought about the young man she'd met so long ago. She'd been smitten almost from the moment she laid eyes on him. He was fun and easy to talk to, and he understood her like no one ever had.

Even as a young woman, she recognized a gentleness and compassion that would make him a wonderful doctor.

She glanced up the street. What if he hadn't received her letter? That didn't negate the fact that he'd betrayed her. And the pain of that wound left a jagged scar on her heart.

Like Taryn said, though, people change. She certainly wasn't the same person Trent met all those years ago.

She blew out a breath. Losing her mother as a little girl, her father six months before her high school graduation... To say she'd been angry with God was an understatement.

Yet He'd restored her faith and given her the greatest blessing of all.

Her gaze collided with Trent's. How would they even begin to forge a friendship?

Austin.

As her son started toward her, Trent turned and crossed the street in the opposite direction. Hands jammed in his pockets, his shoulders were slumped, his gaze downcast.

Her heart went out to him.

"Hey, short man." She held her arms open expectantly.

"Hi, Mom."

She dropped a kiss atop Austin's head, enjoying his all-too-brief embrace. "How was your day?"

He lifted a shoulder. "Okay."

"Then why do you look so down?"

His fluid eyes met hers. "Trent said he can't come to my party."

Blakely felt like someone had slashed her tires. This was her fault. She'd taken aim at Trent's heart and let her arrow fly.

Though the direct hit hadn't brought near the satisfaction she expected.

"Did he say why?"

Austin shook his head, his frown reminding her of Gran's words. That it wasn't just about her.

But it was up to her to make it right.

Despite his optimism, the ache in Trent's heart throbbed into the next day. The way Austin's smile dissolved when he told him he couldn't attend his birthday party had Trent seriously rethinking the decision. But given the sour ending to his last conversation with Blakely, he figured it best to bow out until they could come to some sort of agreement.

When that might happen, though, was anybody's guess. So he was shocked to find a message waiting for him at the clinic the next day. Even more so when she'd asked him to meet her at the church that evening.

Now he waited in the small, empty sanctuary that smelled of lemon oil.

He shifted in the back pew, watching the light fade behind the stained glass windows. What if Blakely had decided not to tell Austin who he was? What if she didn't want him seeing Austin at all? Could she do that? And if she did, how far was Trent willing to go to ensure a place in his son's life? Paternity tests. Court battles. What would that do to Austin?

The rapid-fire questions came to a halt when the front door of the church groaned open. Gentle footfalls trailed down the hall. Closer.

"Hi." A nervous smile flitted across Blakely's face as she

settled into the pew in front of him. "These are for you." She held out a disposable plastic container.

Accepting the package, he peered inside. "Your grandmother's peanut butter cookies." Rose still had his back. "She didn't have to do this."

"Um…she didn't."

"You made these?" He gestured at the container, unable to hide his surprise.

She nodded.

Thoughts whirled again. His gaze narrowed. Was this an olive branch or the calm before the storm?

Recalling all the times she'd brought him cookies that summer, he softened. "Thank you."

"You're welcome."

Silence filled the subsequent moments, as though both seemed afraid to move past the small talk.

He focused on the cross over the baptismal; she kept her head bowed.

"I owe you an apology." Her words were barely above a whisper.

"For what?" He was the one who'd broken faith with her. And all these years she'd believed he'd chosen Lauren and their child over her and Austin. The thought made him sick.

"I was very harsh with you the other day."

"By speaking the truth?"

"Perhaps." She absently traced a figure eight on the ridge of the pew. "Although I know things aren't always what they seem."

When she finally looked at him, he saw understanding in her blue eyes. Or maybe resignation.

"Blakely, you're going to have to cut me some slack here. I'm a guy. We don't always get things. Exactly what are you saying?"

"I'm willing to believe you never got my letter. That you didn't know about Austin."

"*Willing* to believe or you *do* believe? There's a big difference."

Her gaze drifted away. She inhaled deeply. Exhaled, searching him out once again. "I believe you. The man I knew would never have turned his back on Austin."

"Or you," he added, unable to help himself.

Her lips pursed. She swallowed. "Whatever the case, I want you to come to Austin's party."

"You do?"

Had he not been watching her every move, he'd have missed the subtle nod. "It's important to him."

"And you?"

Straightening, she regarded him full-on. "Whatever is important to my son is important to me. The best birthday present he could receive is meeting his father."

Did she have any idea how much her words meant? "You think so?"

"I know so."

He fell against the back of the pew, reality gradually seeping into his thick head. He used to dream of meeting his father. Had Austin had those same dreams? Would learning Trent was his dad be a dream come true, or would it rock Austin's stable world?

"Okay. So how do we do this?"

She puffed out a laugh. "I have no idea."

Thirty minutes later they sat in Rose's living room. Blakely's grandmother excused herself as Blakely joined Austin and Jethro on the beige sofa. Trent perched on the matching loveseat, Ellie Mae collapsed at his feet.

Temps outside were in the low fifties, but sweat still beaded his brow. He swiped clammy palms over his denim-clad thighs.

"Am I in trouble?" Austin tugged Jethro closer, his worried look drifting between Trent and Blakely.

"No, sweetie." She rested a loving hand on the boy's leg. "We just need to talk to you about something."

"Okay." The kid still looked scared to death. But with their grim expressions, what did they expect?

Trent made a lame attempt at a smile. The steady tick-tock of the grandfather clock across the room seemed to accentuate the seriousness of the moment. He rubbed Ellie Mae, gladly accepting whatever comfort the dog offered.

About the time he thought he couldn't wait one more minute, Blakely said, "Honey, Trent is your father."

Excitement and disappointment were the first emotions to cross the boy's face. "You're my...dad?"

"I am."

His son slouched against the overstuffed cushion, pondering the news. "How come you didn't tell me?"

Blakely must have caught Trent's panicked expression because she came to his rescue. "He didn't know, Austin."

Confusion muddied the boy's innocent features. "How come?"

She sighed. "Austin, that's a really long story. One with a lot of miscommunication."

As she broke things down into Austin-size pieces, Trent couldn't help thinking what an amazing woman she was. One that could easily capture his heart again. With all the stuff between them, she still managed to put her son's needs above her own desires. Not everyone would do that.

"Austin, there's only one thing I've ever wanted more than being a doctor, and that's a family. If I had known about you, I would have been here."

"So...does this mean you and Mom are getting married?"

"Well—"

"No." Blakely adjusted a stack of magazines on the coffee table. "Trent and I haven't seen each other in ten years. We barely know each other."

"But, you could get married? Later."

Trent liked the way the kid thought. "This is a big shock for all of us. It'll take time to adjust. I want to know everything about you, Austin. And I'm sure you're going to want to get to know me, too."

"Yeah. So we can still hang out?" He squirmed to the edge of the cushion.

"I'm counting on it, bud."

"What about Mom? Can she hang out with us?"

"If she wants to." Judging from the way Blakely was fidgeting, though, Trent doubted she'd be on board with that. "The most important thing I want you to know right now is that I love you, son, and I will always be here for you."

"Can I call you Dad?"

Trent managed to speak around the lump in his throat. "I would be honored to have you call me Dad."

"Okay. Dad." Austin's grin was so big his cheeks would probably hurt tomorrow. "This is so cool. Mom, can I call Zach and tell him?"

Her reaction was a little more reserved. She smoothed a hand over his hair. "Go ahead."

Austin leaped to his feet and charged toward the rolltop desk. He grabbed the cordless handset and bounded up the stairs.

Forearms on his knees, Trent looked at Blakely. "You've just given me the greatest gift of my life. Thank you."

"I heard someone running upstairs." Rose approached from the office, her concerned gaze darting between Trent and Blakely. "How'd it go?"

"He couldn't wait to call Zach, if that tells you anything." Blakely pushed to her feet.

"Oh." A relieved smile blossomed on Rose's face. "Well, I guess everything went all right, then."

"Yes, it did." Trent stood and stretched, watching Blakely cross the room, arms wound around her midsection in a protective mode. If only it were so easy to gain her trust. Regardless of what she said, he recognized the hurt embedded below the surface. Hurt that only time, persistence and the Good Lord's grace could overcome.

And when she finds out you're leaving?

Good thing he wasn't one to give up without a fight. Because Blakely Daniels was definitely worth fighting for.

Chapter Nine

"That's awesome, Mr. Burk. Thank you for calling." Blakely did a little happy dance as she hung up the phone at the front desk. News that the parts for her damaged vehicle had arrived early was the best she'd had all week. According to Mr. Burk, an old friend of Granddad's from the body shop in Montrose, she should have the truck by next weekend.

With a definite spring in her step, she scurried around the counter and went back to unpacking a shipment of T-shirts that had arrived in time for the long holiday weekend. A good weekend it was setting up to be, too. All but one of her rental Jeeps had been reserved and there was limited seating on most of Saturday's tours. Sunday was filling up just as quickly, so she'd already decided to call Tomboy—a four-door Jeep 4 X 4 with a jump seat in the back—into action should the need arise.

She admired one of the new men's shirts. Electric pink with black lettering with the Adventures in Pink logo on the left breast and *Real Men Aren't Afraid of Pink* emblazoned on the back. Her favorite. Though for the less adventurous males, she had black shirts with pink lettering.

The front door swung open and Blakely turned to greet her guest. Her smile evaporated when she spotted Ross Chapman.

"It's after six o'clock. Shouldn't you be getting home to

your family?" He continued across the blue-gray carpet and fingered one of the shirts. "Cute."

The man could set off her Irish temper faster than anyone she'd ever known. A fact she was determined to keep to herself.

"I don't see how that's any of your business, Ross." She folded another shirt, trying to keep her frustration at bay. She set the shirt atop the previous one.

"Come on. We both know your grandmother's not a young woman."

Blakely couldn't help but chuckle. "Don't let her hear you say that."

"Nonetheless, with old Bill gone, somebody needs to look out for her. Not to mention that boy of yours."

"I'm sure we can manage just fine."

He shrugged. "Just sayin'."

"Did you drop by for anything in particular or merely to instruct me on how to care for my family?"

"As a matter of fact, I did." He rubbed his carefully trimmed beard. "I've been thinking. I wasn't exactly fair last week." He scrutinized every nuance of the room, ratcheting her anxiety. No telling what kind of mental notes the guy was taking.

"I'd like to up my offer for Adventures in Pink." He threw out an obscene amount.

Puffing out a disbelieving laugh, she added the last shirt to the pile. "I'm sorry, Ross. The answer is the same. Adventures in Pink is *not* for sale."

"Aw, come on now, missy. Everybody's got a price."

Like Dale Hannon. After a handful of visits to Ouray, Ross decided he wanted his own tour company. Made old man Hannon an offer he couldn't refuse.

She wasn't old man Hannon.

She crossed her arms over her chest. "There are some things money can't buy."

"You say that now. But suppose something happened to that boy of yours, or your grandmother took ill. Do you take care of them or take care of business? If you choose them, who'll manage things here?"

"I guess that's something I'll have to figure out if and when the time comes."

"By then it may be too late. Offers like mine don't hang around forever."

No, but he certainly did.

"I'll keep that in mind, Ross." She picked up the empty cardboard box. "Now, if you don't mind, I need to finish up so I can get home to my family."

The red in his cheeks indicated he wasn't pleased with her answer. He started toward the door. Paused. "Can we be honest here?" He cast her one of those smiles meant to charm.

Instead, it grated her nerves.

"I'm trying to help you out, Blakely. You're the best tour guide around. You love these mountains." He pointed a manicured—yes, manicured—nail in her direction. "But you don't know the first thing about running a business. It's a tough job. Money can get pretty tight sometimes. Don't let your stubbornness stand in the way of what's really important."

By now, she was about to bite her tongue in two. Tears burned the backs of her eyes and she was sure her own face was at least two shades redder than Ross's.

"Good night, Ross." With that, she turned, stormed down the five steps that led to the garage and plowed right into Trent.

Trent had to tell Blakely that he was only here for the summer. The more honest he was, the better off things would be.

But one look at her told him this wasn't the time. Steam practically poured from her ears. He could only hope that exasperation wasn't directed at him.

He palmed her shoulders. "You don't look so good."

Tears trailed down her cheeks. Instinctively, he pulled her into his arms.

"Hey, now. What's wrong?" With her head nestled perfectly under his chin, he peered through the glass and saw Ross Chapman on his way out the front door.

Trent's own anger rallied. "Did Ross do something to upset you?"

For a moment, she leaned into him and he reveled in the feel of her. The fruity scent of her shampoo.

Her breath hitched. Then she pulled away. "No. I'm okay." She sniffed and wiped the back of her hand across her cheek. "If you're looking for Austin, he's already gone home."

"I'm kind of surprised you're not with him. It's almost seven."

She glared at him. "What? You think I can't run Adventures in Pink and take care of Austin, too? I suppose you think I should be with him one hundred percent of the time."

What set that off?

He threw his hands up in surrender. "Whoa! I wasn't suggesting that at all. You're just usually gone by this time."

Her shoulders slumped. "I know. Big weekend ahead, though."

"So it seems. Every place in town has been sprucing up." He pointed to the cardboard box in her hand.

"Unpacking some new shirts." She flattened the box.

"Can I see?"

"Sure." She tossed it into a recycling container on her way inside.

He followed, immediately noticing two things. The bright pink shirts and the fact that Blakely was quick to flip the closed sign and shut the front door. Again, he wondered why Chapman upset her so. This was the third time he'd seen them interact, and each time Blakely seemed shaken to the core.

"What do you think?" She unfurled one of the pink shirts. Rotated it. "Brand-new design."

Not bad. Still, he lifted a brow, hoping to lighten the mood. "These are for guys?"

"They are. So what do you say? Are you man enough to wear pink?"

"Hey, I might be afraid to drive these mountain roads, but I happen to look very good in pink."

That earned him a smile. A beautiful one that highlighted the silver flecks in her eyes.

"Good." She tossed it to him. "This one's on the house."

"Cool." He slid it on over his T-shirt, struck a pose and summoned his best Donald Duck voice. "How do I look?"

Her laugh was amazing.

"Best advertising I've ever had."

"Good. I'll wear it every chance I get." As he watched her roam about, closing garage doors, shutting down computers and flipping off lights, the urge to protect her sliced through him like a scalpel.

"Blakely, I'm not trying to butt into your business, but is Ross Chapman giving you problems? Because if he is, I'll be happy to step in."

She turned away from the computer at the main desk, the corners of her mouth lifting a notch. "Thank you. That's very sweet. But it's just business." She clicked the shutdown icon and stepped away from the counter. "He…doesn't seem to like some of the choices I've made." Retrieving a pink and black tote bag from a file drawer, she fished out a set of keys and kicked the drawer shut with her foot. "But they're not his to make, so he's going to have to deal with it. Are you ready?"

Okay, so she wasn't comfortable confiding in him.

Not that he was doing any better.

He followed her out the front door and waited as she twisted the key in the lock.

"Sorry for going off on you in the shop." She started down the steps. "I never even gave you a chance to explain why you were here."

"Oh, that." He let go a nervous laugh as they continued toward the alley across the street. "I, uh…" No, this wasn't the time. "I'm planning a run to Montrose in the morning to pick up a new door for your grandmother. Would it be okay for Austin to join me?"

Chapter Ten

Blakely stepped from her Jeep at Hot Springs Park determined to put the struggles of the day behind her. The sweet aroma of fresh-mown grass told her she couldn't have hand-picked better weather for Austin's party. Unseasonably warm temperatures had much of the day bordering on uncomfortable. But now that the sun had dipped behind Twin Peaks, the shade-cooled air was beyond perfect.

"Austin, will you grab that tote while I get your presents?" She pointed to the large bag that contained party favors and towels situated beside her son.

"Okay." He lugged the carryall behind him as he emerged from the backseat. "What about my cake?"

"Don't you worry, Austin." Gran slid out the passenger side. "Taryn will have your cake here in plenty of time."

He shadowed Blakely to the rear of the vehicle. "You sure you don't need help carrying *all* those presents?" His charming demeanor failed to draw Blakely in. This time.

"Oh, no you don't, short man." She faced him, one hand on her hip, the other on the spare tire. "I'll tell you what, though. You can carry them when we leave."

"Aw, Mom." Unruffled, he scuffed across the gravel parking lot while she retrieved a laundry basket full of wrapped gifts from the back of the Jeep. As usual, she'd gone overboard. But when it came to her son, she couldn't seem to help herself.

"Would you care to tell me what's bothering you?" Gran studied her with a knowing eye.

The old gal's intuitiveness was hard to escape. Blakely knew she'd be hard-pressed to hide her distress. Though that wasn't about to stop her from trying.

"There's nothing bothering me."

"Blakely, I've known you all your life. I *know* when you're upset."

Sick was more like it. But this was Austin's special day. She wouldn't let her less-than-perfect life ruin his celebration.

Brightly wrapped gifts in hand, she shoved the back gate closed with her hip as Taryn pulled alongside them.

"What's going on, ladies?"

"Blakely's upset."

Her head swung toward her grandmother. "I am not."

"Ooo-kay." Taryn eased from her Jeep, her gaze fixed on Blakely. "So would somebody like to explain?"

"You two are unbelievable." Blakely tempered her voice. "I will *not* ruin Austin's day."

"Which is exactly why you should get whatever is bothering you off your chest." Taryn inched beside Gran.

"Oh, good grief." She may as well dump. The whole town would know by tomorrow anyway. "I lost one of my guides."

"Which one?" Suddenly understanding, her grandmother frowned.

"Bruce."

The furrow between Gran's brows deepened. "He's been with us for years."

"His wife lost her job," said Taryn.

"Yeah. So when Ross Chapman offered to double his income, well…"

Taryn's mouth formed a perfect *O* before she pressed her lips together. "Well, that stinks." She started around the passenger side, giving Blakely a we'll-talk-later look. "But, like you said, this is Austin's day. And I've got a fudge marble cake that's guaranteed to improve anybody's mood." She lifted the foil-covered board from the front seat.

Blakely gasped. "Taryn, that's amazing." She and Gran both moved closer. "This must have taken forever." A quarter-sheet cake served as a backboard that read "Happy Birthday Austin," while an orange-iced basketball mounded neatly in a frosting net. "How on earth did you do that?"

Taryn wrinkled her nose. "Do you think he'll like it?"

Looking at her friend, Blakely knew this creation was born of love. Not only for Austin, but for the child she never knew.

"Nope. I think he's gonna love it. Come on, let's show him."

The trio followed the path Austin had taken across the lush green grass to the playground adjacent to the hot springs pool. Red, green and blue balloons swayed from a covered picnic table boasting a reserved sign.

"That looks like our spot," said Blakely.

Austin waited beside the green plastic-coated table. "Can I get in the pool now?"

"No, you may not." Blakely lay the basket on a nearby bench. "Not until all your guests are here. Besides, I think Miss Taryn has something you'll want to see."

His eyes widened at the sight of the confectionary master-piece. "Is that for me?"

"Well, it has your name on it." Pleasure brightened Taryn's beautiful face.

"Wow! This is going to be the coolest party ever."

Staring out over the soccer field, Blakely spied a familiar face. "There's Zach."

Austin sprinted to greet his friend, and the poor kid only grew antsier with each guest who arrived. He was ready to hit that pool.

Blakely could certainly relate. Gran and Granddad used to claim she was part fish. And though they'd never admitted it, she had a sneaking suspicion that's why they installed the pool at The Alps. That way, when she spent her summers here, she could swim until her heart's content, and they never had to leave the motel.

None too soon for Austin, his friends were all accounted for. Everyone except Trent, that is, though she knew he'd be along as soon as he could break away from the medical clinic. She'd never seen anyone worry so much over a birthday present, but Trent had picked her brain relentlessly. She could hardly wait to see what he decided.

"Blakes." Taryn nudged her as they watched the kids play on the waterslides. "Why don't you get in some laps? I can hang with the kids."

The larger hot springs pool was divided into smaller sections for work, play or relaxation. And right now, a good workout would go a long way toward relieving some stress.

"You sure you don't mind?"

"I wouldn't have offered if I did. Now go."

Two laps into her workout, Blakely realized how badly she needed the exercise. Slowly, but surely, the tension flowed from the muscles between her shoulder blades. She picked up the pace, eager to erase the residue of Ross's shenanigans.

Warm water rushed over her body, taking with it the stress of the past few weeks. Telling Austin the truth about Trent had been the right thing to do. Though that was only a few days ago, it seemed the news had filled a void she didn't even know Austin had.

She paused at one end to catch her breath.

"Easy there, champ. You'll be too tuckered to party."

She jerked her head up.

Trent hovered over her, looking blue and a bit foggy. She lifted her goggles and stared up at him. He looked incredible, while she looked…like a drowned rat.

"Ready to join the kids?" He extended his hand, his smile creating a chink in the wall she'd built around her heart.

His biceps flexed as he lifted her out of the water, reminding her how it felt to be held in those strong arms. Safe. Protected.

Vulnerable.

Straightening, she peeled off the goggles. "Let's go."

"Mom! Dad!" Austin hollered as they approached the play pool. "Watch this." He dove beneath the water and performed a perfectly straight handstand before reemerging.

"Nice one," said Trent.

"Did Austin just say 'Dad'?"

So much for stress relief.

Turning, Blakely came face-to-face with Nicole Chapman.

For the briefest of moments, laughter, conversation and the sound of splashing water swirled around Blakely in a maddening cacophony. The secret she'd held for so long had finally come to light. Despite the intensity of her workout, she willed her breathing to even.

"Hello, Nicole." Blakely's gaze landed on the equally blonde Mary Chapman, Nicole's mother. "Mary." She gestured to Trent, realizing she'd better get used to the surprised looks and questioning stares. "I'd like you to meet Trent Lockridge, Austin's father."

"I knew it!" Nicole's gaze surfed Trent with an air of appreciation. "Now we know where Austin got his good looks."

Something coiled in the pit of Blakely's stomach.

She looked for Taryn. Spotted her playing with the kids on the other side of the pool.

"I will take that as a compliment," Trent said, seemingly indifferent to her admiration.

"You should." Mary waggled her drawn-on eyebrows.

Water pelted the quartet. The Chapman women shrieked.

"Are you guys gonna get in?" Austin aimed another spray of water at his father.

Smiling, Trent regarded the women again. "Ladies, you'll have to excuse us. We're celebrating our son's birthday."

Blakely tried not to think about how good his hand felt at the small of her back as he guided her toward the pool.

"Blakely, honey." Mary touched Blakely's elbow, halting her retreat. "Ross told me about your driver." Her syrupy Southern drawl accentuated an exaggerated pout. "I'm so sorry. When it comes to business, that man of mine will do almost anything."

Blakely knew good and well Mary wasn't any more sorry about Ross stealing Bruce than she was about Austin splashing them. Well, two can play at that game.

Covering Mary's hand with her own, Blakely dug deep for her sweetest voice. "The term is *guide,* Mary. And no worries. It's just business."

Trent continued to urge her down the steps, into the steaming water. Of all the people they could have run into. If Trent hadn't been with her, no telling how she would have reacted. Instead, his presence helped her step boldly out of her comfort zone.

"What is it with that family?" Trent's whisper had chill bumps erupting down her wet arms.

"Money." Sinking beneath the surface, she observed Mary and Nicole as they strolled away. Their ever-present smiles never seemed to reach their eyes. "Enough to buy almost anything they want."

"Except happiness."

She stared at Trent. "Very perceptive, doctor."

Austin swam between them, then circled around Blakely before breaking the surface. When he did, he pounced on her back, trying with all his might to dunk her.

"Need a little help there, buddy?"

"Oh, no you d—"

Before she could get the words out, Trent seized her around the waist and tossed her into the air. She sucked in a quick breath as the water drew ever closer.

A split second later the warm liquid bubbled and gurgled around her. She broke through the surface, pushing hair out of her face. Opening her eyes, she saw Austin, his mouth agape, a smile niggling at the corners. Trent, however, grinned from ear to ear, arms folded across his hulking chest in a satisfied manner. Just like he'd done all those summers ago.

A lifeguard's whistle rent the air, and Trent's head whipped in the direction of the sound.

"No horseplay." The teenage boy quickly resumed his post.

Blakely swiped at the water dripping from her nose, uncertain how she felt about the playful interaction. Once upon a time, she would have reveled in it. Even retaliated. Now?

"You are in so much trouble, mister."

"Promises, promises." The playful edge to his voice made her heart stutter.

But warning sirens blared in her head. *Retreat! Retreat!*

Turning her attention to Taryn, Austin and his stunned friends, she said, "All right, gang. About twenty minutes and it'll be time for pizza."

"Yay!" They cheered in unison.

Then, without acknowledging Trent, she exited the pool.

By the time she'd changed clothes and made it back to the picnic area, Trent was waiting beside Gran, dressed and holding a bouquet of flowers.

A peace offering, no doubt. How he'd managed to come up with them on such short notice was puzzling to say the least.

Refusing to look at him, Blakely snatched the tote bag and pulled out the papergoods.

"I am so sorry, Blakely." He stood behind her now. "I don't know what came over me."

"Don't worry. It was all in fun."

"I know, but I was out of line back there. I set a bad example for those kids."

Nodding, Blakely set a basketball-themed plate and napkin at each place. "Yes. Yes, you did."

At the end of the table, Gran looked appalled, but Blakely knew better. "Young man, just exactly what did you do?"

He shifted back and forth. "Ma'am. I, uh, well, I dunked your granddaughter."

Blakely whirled. "Dunked? That was way more than a dunking. You tossed me halfway across the pool."

"Oh, it wasn't that far."

Gran feigned indignation, pressing a hand to her chest. "Of all times—" her expression softened "—times for me to be without a camera." The old gal chuckled. "Trent, you should see the look on your face."

Blakely burst into laughter. "Gotcha!"

Grinning, he raked a hand through his hair. "Okay. I deserved that." Then, as though he suddenly remembered the flowers, he held them out. "These are for you."

Accepting the tissue-wrapped package, she inhaled the fragrance of white tulips and bright pink roses. "What are these for?"

"Well…" His nervousness was endearing. "It may be Austin's birthday, but he wouldn't be here without you. You did all the work. Thank you."

Another piece of her wall crumbled. "They're beautiful." Cradling the bouquet against her chest, she turned and rapidly blinked away the moisture threatening to disarm her. She couldn't remember the last time someone had done something so sweet. So…romantic.

No, red roses were romance. Pink…?

These roses were the exact shade of her Jeeps. And the white tulips…

He remembered.

She sucked in a fortifying breath. "I wish I had something to put them in."

He stared at her with that lopsided smile that used to send her over the moon.

Gran admired the bouquet. "They'll be fine until we get home."

"Is the pizza ready?"

How long had Austin been there?

"Pizza?" She handed Gran the flowers. "Yes. I was just going to get them."

Behind the kids, Taryn grinned at Blakely. Add this to the list of things they'd be talking about later.

"Taryn, would you mind adding a goodie bag to each place setting?"

"Sure thing."

With Trent at her side, Blakely hurried in the direction of the Snack Shack. She was used to taking care of things by herself, so his presence had her on edge. Or maybe it was his actions. So much like the heroes in all those romance novels she read.

But this is real life. She'd been burned before. Enough to know not to play with fire.

"What happened to your guide?"

She'd hoped he hadn't heard Mary. But, of course, he had. He was right there with her.

Dodging two preschool boys enjoying a hearty game of chase around the twisting slide, she pondered her response.

"*One* of my guides." Her best one. "He quit."

"And went to work for Ross, I gather."

She quietly nodded, not wanting her annoyance to resurface.

"Does that put you in a bind?"

They rounded the corner of the Snack Shack. "Maybe. I haven't figured it out yet."

"Hey there, Blakely."

"Tiffany." She leaned against the wood counter. "I didn't expect to see you back so soon. You home for the summer?"

"Yes, ma'am."

"Austin will be happy to see you." Prior to leaving for college, Tiffany had been his favorite babysitter.

"Is he enjoying his party?"

"Oh, you know him. He's got his friends, the water…what more could a little guy ask for? Except maybe pizza. Are they ready?"

Tiffany glanced toward the kitchen. "Almost." Turning back, she looked past Blakely. "May I help you?"

"I'm with her." Trent pointed a thumb in Blakely's direction.

She hesitated. An introduction was in order, but the words stuck in her throat.

"Here you go." A teenage boy saved her by dropping four large pizza boxes on the counter. "Hot and ready to go."

Tiffany rang up the amount, and Trent stepped forward, his wallet in hand. "May I?"

Blakely liked that he asked. "Be my guest."

She saw the way Tiffany watched them. The way her questioning gaze studied Trent.

Oh, yeah. Blakely was going to be making lots and lots of introductions.

Over his thirty years, Trent had learned that the greatest joy often came from the simplest things. Like singing "Happy Birthday" to his son for the first time in his life.

With a belly full of pizza and fudge marble cake, Trent hovered near the picnic table and watched Austin open his presents, silently praising God for the gift *he'd* been given. He appreciated the fact that, no matter how big or small, the boy acted as though each gift was his favorite, something to be treasured.

When the toys had all been unwrapped, Trent took a small, rectangular package from his shirt pocket and handed it to his son.

"Thanks." Austin didn't attack the gift with the same gusto as the others. Instead, he carefully tore off the red wrapping, as though he suspected something precious lay within.

Trent hoped he didn't let him down. He'd had the hardest time deciding what to get. Nothing felt right. He prayed Austin would like it. Maybe he should have gone for one of the toys Blakely mentioned.

With the paper gone, Austin lifted the lid. "A pocket knife! All right!"

"It, uh…" Trent cleared his throat. "It was my father's." The pearl-handled knife was the only remnant he had of his father. After all the foster homes Trent had been in, it was amazing he still had it.

He could hear the awe in the kid's voices.

"Cool," one said.

"That must be an antique," another added. Even Blakely laughed at that one.

Moving to the other side of the table where she stood, Trent leaned toward her, hands shoved in his pockets. "I hope you don't mind. But, if you're worried, I'll tell him it's for display only."

"That knife was your most cherished possession." Compassion swam in those blue eyes.

"It was. But Austin means far more."

She gazed up at him, a delicate smile playing on her full lips. "You did great."

The approval in her voice was balm to his wounded heart. He hoped for that same approval when she learned he was leaving.

He had to tell her tonight.

The rosy-red light of the alpenglow had settled over the Amphitheater by the time parents arrived to collect their children. To Trent's surprise, Blakely introduced him to each one. Something he knew didn't come easy, which made him appreciate her all the more.

By the time the last child left, Taryn had everything gathered and ready to go. Trent grabbed what he could carry and still offered his arm to Rose. The old gal appeared to have run out of steam, sitting at the picnic table, looking dazed. He wouldn't have thought the event too much for her, but maybe he'd misjudged.

"Can I help you to the car?" He offered his free hand.

"Thank you, Trent." The old woman's grip seemed unusually weak as she struggled to stand.

Pulling her toward him, he hooked her arm through his. "Are you feeling okay, Mrs. D?"

Blakely's pointed glance told him she'd heard his question.

She handed Austin a laundry basket mounded with his gifts. "Why don't you escort Miss Taryn to her car?"

"Okay. Can I ride home with Dad?"

"Fine by me," Trent offered, wanting the opportunity to not only observe Rose, but talk with Blakely.

The birthday boy trotted away with Taryn, chattering about his totally awesome cake.

"Everything okay?" Blakely took hold of her grandmother's other arm.

"I don't know what's wrong with me." Rose shuffled along the path as though her legs were weighted. "I feel so…woozy."

Blakely's worried gaze found his, silently pleading for him to do something. And although he doubted it was anything serious, he wasn't about to take any chances.

"Let's get her home."

Chapter Eleven

Blakely refused to entertain the thought of losing another loved one. Yet there it was.

Not now. Please, not now.

After situating her grandmother into the Jeep, Trent caught Blakely by the arm. "Was she having any problems earlier?"

"No." Panic swirled in her gut. She tried to temper it, but to no avail. "This isn't like her at all. Should I take her to the hospital?"

"I don't think that's necessary. My medical bag is in the car. I'll have a look at her once we get to the house." Taking her hand in his, he softened his expression. "It could have been something she ate."

If he hadn't been here, Blakely was sure she'd be in a heap on the ground about now. Her gratitude morphed into a sad smile. "I appreciate that."

By the time they returned to the motel, Gran's fair skin was paler than normal and she found it difficult to stand as Trent helped her out of the Jeep.

Blakely helped him settle the older woman on the sofa. Per Trent's instruction, Austin was quick to intercept the dogs and put them outside.

"Thank you, sweetie." Blakely caressed his back, trying to keep a calm face.

"Is Gran gonna be okay?" Though Austin had been at school when Granddad had his heart attack, the fallout had still been hard on him.

She stroked his soft curls. "Don't you worry. Trent will take good care of her." Of that, she was sure.

Trent glanced up at her. "Does she take any medication?"

"Yes—for high blood pressure."

"Anything else?"

Arms wrapped around herself, she shook her head, gaze riveted to her grandmother.

Trent opened his backpack and pulled out a stethoscope. Calm. Cool.

"Mrs. D, I'm going to do a quick examination. Make sure everything is all right."

She nodded, her lips almost white.

He ripped open the blood pressure cuff and wrapped it around Gran's arm. Setting the stethoscope in the crook of her elbow, he squeezed the bulb until the Velcro crackled in protest.

His brow furrowed. "You say she's being treated for high blood pressure?"

"Yes." Blakely didn't want to feel the fear coursing through her. "Why?"

Ripping the Velcro apart, he removed the cuff. "Her blood pressure's a bit low. Nothing alarming, though."

"What could cause that? I mean, is that what's making her feel bad?" She needed to calm down before Austin picked up on her growing concern. But calm didn't come naturally in situations like this. Not when she'd already lost most everyone she'd ever loved.

"Mrs. D? When did you last take your blood pressure medication?"

Her grandmother kept her eyes closed. "At the party. Before we ate."

Blakely scrolled through her mental files. That wasn't right. "No, Gran. You took it before we left the house. Don't you remember?"

Trent turned his attention to Blakely. "Are you sure?"

"Yes. I watched her take it about thirty minutes before we left."

"Mrs. D, could you have taken your medication twice?"

"I...don't know." She sounded so weak. "I took it at the park with a sip of the kids' soda pop."

"So she took it twice?" Blakely felt the color leach from her face. Why hadn't she monitored her grandmother more closely? "Is that bad?"

"Drops the blood pressure lower than normal. Like I said, not alarming, but it can definitely make one feel out of sorts." He placed a finger on Gran's wrist, checking her pulse. "Blakely, would you bring me something with caffeine, please? Coffee or tea."

"What? How can you think of drinks at a time like this?" Some bedside manner.

Trent glanced up at her. "Your grandmother needs a mild stimulant."

"Oh." Blakely's cheeks grew hotter by the nanosecond. "Will that bring her blood pressure back up?"

"That and some rest. Yes."

Austin tilted his head to look at Blakely. "So, Gran's gonna be okay?"

"By tomorrow she should be good as new," said Trent.

Her boy plucked the hunter-green afghan from the loveseat and covered his grandmother's legs. "You hear that, Gran? Dad's gonna get you all fixed up."

Relief spilled through Blakely as she went into the kitchen to make some of Gran's favorite tea. *Thank You, Lord. Thank You.*

With trembling hands, she filled a mug with water and added a tea bag. Water slopped over the sides as she aimed for the microwave.

"Looks like you could use a little help yourself." Smiling, Trent took the cup from her, the slight touch of his fingers sending a tingling sensation up her arm and straight to her heart. He put the cup inside the microwave, punched the buttons, then stood in front of her. "You're pretty shaken."

She dodged around him, grabbed the rag from the sink and wiped up the water she'd spilled. "I'm fine."

"No, you're not."

She knew she shouldn't have looked at him, but she did anyway. The tenderness in those deep brown eyes made her want to throw herself into his arms and absorb his strength.

If that wouldn't scream desperate, she didn't know what would.

"Okay, so I was a little rattled."

"A little?"

"All right, a lot." She laid the rag beside the sink and took a deep, calming breath. "Thank you for being here. For being—"

"A doctor."

Actually, she was going to say wonderful, but his response was safer.

She let out a soft laugh. "Yes, thank you for being a doctor."

The microwave beeped and Trent grabbed the hot mug. "Why don't I carry this?"

As he left the room, Blakely wondered what she would have done if he hadn't been here. Seemed the more he was around, the more she wanted him around. But that meant putting her heart on the line. And that's what scared her most.

Trent could hardly wait to spend another evening with his son. He looked forward to each and every moment with Austin, tucking away the memories, praying that they would sustain him when he went back to Albuquerque.

Walking the streets of Ouray Thursday evening, they could hear the music long before they made it to Fellin Park. When they did, it was obvious the festival was in full swing. People scattered across the lawn on blankets and lawn chairs. Some even danced in front of the stage as a country-rock band belted out their rendition of "Sweet Home Alabama."

With his boy at his side, Trent trekked across the grass, the aromas from numerous food vendors making his mouth water.

He leaned toward Austin. "Are you hungry?"

"Starving."

He ruffled the kid's hair. "That's what you always say."

His boy shrugged. "'Cause it's always true."

Trent chuckled. That growth spurt should be kicking in anytime.

"Look. There's Mom." Austin pointed to a grouping of tents off to one side.

Clad in an Adventures in Pink T-shirt, a smiling Blakely offered up hamburgers alongside her friend Taryn.

Trent's conscience nudged him. He'd planned to tell her the truth the other night. Then Rose took ill and his plans evaporated.

Thankfully, she was back to her old chipper self by the next morning. Still… It seemed whenever he made plans to come clean, God put something in his path to stop him. He guessed he'd just have to be patient and wait for the right time.

Not that he expected Blakely to have a problem with his departure. But his desire to have Austin spend holidays and summers with him in New Mexico would likely send her into a tizzy.

"Come on, Dad. Let's get something to eat." Austin took off through the small sea of people.

Trent followed. That is, until Ross Chapman stopped him. Held out his hand.

"Evening, Dr. Lockridge."

"Ross." Trent accepted the gesture, his gaze still trained on his son.

"Looks like that young fellow's in a mighty big hurry."

"Yeah, there's not much that stands between a growing boy and his food."

Hands on his hips, Ross shifted his focus back to Trent. "So where's his mother?"

He nodded in the direction of the vendors, eager to be there with Austin. "Blakely volunteered to help out."

Ross shook his head. "It's no wonder she's losing business."

"Excuse me?" Trent jerked his attention to Ross.

"Bless her heart. That one's got so many irons in the fire. What with the high season upon us and so little time to spend with her boy."

"Are you kidding? Blakely spends more time with Austin than many two-parent families."

"Don't get me wrong. She's a fine mother. And now that you're here to help her..." Ross chuckled. "That is, if she'll let you. She's one stubborn filly, isn't she?"

Trent crossed his arms over his chest and glared down at the man. "And you would know that how?"

Ross shrugged. "Business dealings." He leaned closer, pretending to survey the ever-growing crowd. "Just between you and me, she's got an offer on the table."

"Offer? For what?"

"Adventures in Pink."

A disbelieving laugh blew out before Trent could stop it. "Are you kidding? She lives and breathes Adventures in Pink. Blakely would never sell."

Ross turned a serious eye Trent's way. "Everyone's got their price."

"Then you don't know Blakely."

"Perhaps. But it would certainly free her up to concentrate on what's really important." Ross glanced toward Austin. "Like that boy of yours." With that, Ross turned on his booted heel and walked away.

Trent balled his fists, then dropped them to his sides. No wonder Blakely got so nervous when Ross was around. The guy was gunning for her business.

Spotting Austin at the hamburger stand, Trent continued in that direction. He dodged around a couple teenagers tossing a Frisbee. Was Blakely really losing business? Not from the looks of things this weekend. From what he could tell, every tour was at capacity.

Still, if money were a problem, it was his duty to help. Granted, most of his funds were tied up in the new practice, but he could offer some assistance.

"You should get a burger, Dad." Austin accepted the paper-wrapped one Taryn handed him, along with a lidded drink.

"They sure smell good," he said, stepping up to the long table that served as a counter.

"I see you were talking to Ross." Blakely's gaze drifted from one thing to the next, her failure to look Trent in the eye speaking volumes about how nervous the encounter made her.

"Unfortunately."

"What did he want?"

Good question. What did Chapman want? To stir up trouble was his best guess. Though his revelations had left one nagging question.

Was Adventures in Pink really in trouble?

Chapter Twelve

Trent had to find someplace else to live.

Sipping his coffee from Mouse's, he wandered along Main Street as the sun lifted above the Amphitheater Saturday morning. He didn't know what his thought process had been when he first arrived in Ouray, but a tiny motel room just wasn't going to cut it any longer.

He paused while someone snapped a picture of the historic Beaumont Hotel, then continued his aimless trek. Of course, when he first arrived, he didn't have a clue about Austin. Now he wanted to spend time with the kid. Hang out with him. That was hard to do in a motel.

What he needed was an apartment. Even a little efficiency apartment would be better than where he was now. Something like where he lived that summer, above Adventures in Pink.

Grinning, he eyed the line of vehicles winding the switchbacks that would carry them into Ouray. Who was he kidding? He stood a better chance of striking it rich in some gold mine than of Blakely renting to him. Assuming she even rented the units anymore. Running a tour company was one thing; acting as a landlord was another.

"Morning." Nodding to a middle-aged couple strolling past,

he glimpsed a painting in the window of the art gallery. He crossed the sidewalk.

More impressionistic, this rendering of Twin Falls didn't have near the depth as Blakely's mural. It lacked the passion and emotion. An image versus a relationship.

Had Blakely put any of her works in a gallery? They'd certainly garner top dollar. And he'd be the first in line.

He stepped back, aware that he was getting off task. An apartment. That was his goal for today.

Doing an about-face, he started in the direction of a real estate office he'd spotted earlier. With any luck, they'd be open soon.

"Dad!"

Turning, he saw Austin jogging toward him. Beside him, Jethro's tiny legs moved at the speed of light.

Trent downed the rest of his coffee, tossed the lidded cup into a trash receptacle and moseyed toward the duo. The delight that danced across Austin's face whenever he saw Trent brought him more joy than he'd ever known.

"You're out bright and early."

His boy smiled up at him. "Gotta get my chores done if I wanna sleep over at Zach's tonight. He's having an end-of-school party."

Ah, yes. The first day of summer break. "So what do you plan on doing with yourself now that school's out?"

Austin shrugged. "I dunno. But at least there won't be homework."

Trent couldn't help but laugh. "That's right. Summers are meant for fun."

They resumed walking at a leisurely pace. Much to Jethro's relief.

"What will your mother and grandmother do without you to keep them in line tonight?"

"Gran's playing cards with her friends. I don't know what

Mom's gonna do. Probably motel stuff since Gran will be gone."

"Oh, really?" Trent couldn't help the slow smile that spread across his face. "That doesn't sound like much fun."

How pathetic. Blakely had a Saturday evening to herself and here she stood doing laundry. She should be treating herself to her favorite meal, watching her favorite movie…or better yet, she should skip the meal and indulge in a sumptuous dessert. Her mouth watered just thinking about a dark chocolate truffle from Mouse's.

She sighed.

Instead, she'd probably end up eating a frozen dinner and reading another romance novel. Definitely pathetic.

Thoughts of Trent drifted across her mind. And, as much as it bothered her, she found herself wondering what he was doing. She couldn't imagine living in a motel room where the only place to stretch out was a bed. No household chores to keep you busy. No way to cook.

Sorting through a pile of Austin's socks, she struggled to find a pair that didn't have holes in them. Good grief. They were only a month old. How did the kid manage to get a hole in every toe? She tossed a handful into the trash. "Time to buy more."

With a laundry basket perched on one hip, Blakely started for the stairs when the bell dinged in the office. Jethro barked but waited for Ellie Mae to lead the way. When she did, her entire midsection swayed back and forth.

Blakely dropped the basket on the couch and followed the canines. "Good eve—" She drew in a sudden breath.

"Anyone up for some ham, pineapple and black olive pizza?" Trent stood on the other side of the counter, next to the brochure rack, holding the flat box in one hand. "And if that's not enough to satisfy your taste buds—" he waggled a smaller box with the other "—we've got a selection of Mouse's finest truffles for dessert."

She wasn't sure what thrilled her more, him or the food.

The dogs danced at his feet, their noses in the air.

Who could blame them? The tantalizing aroma wafted through the small office, making Blakely's stomach growl.

After all these years, he'd remembered her favorite. Usually she had to settle for something else because her family thought pineapple on pizza was weird.

"Omigosh. *That* would be awesome."

His smile did strange things to her insides as she motioned him down the hall and into the dining room. She'd probably regret the move later, but at the moment, her appetite overruled her common sense.

Girl, lighten up for once and have fun.

Where had that come from?

What are you afraid of?

Interesting. What *was* she afraid of?

Falling for Trent. Having her heart ripped out. Again.

Jethro and Ellie Mae pranced about the room as Blakely slid the silk sunflower centerpiece to one end of the table. "I'll get some plates."

"Hey, I'm curious about something." He set the box on the table. "Are you still painting? I mean, other than the mural at Adventures in Pink."

She paused at the cupboard. Outside of her family, no one had ever believed in her talent as much as Trent. He used to tell her she'd be a famous artist one day.

"On occasion." There wasn't time for painting when Austin was little. Once he started school, her desire rekindled. Especially after doing the murals at church and Adventures in Pink. So much so that she'd been working on turning one of the apartments over Adventures in Pink into a studio. A place where she'd have room to work and wouldn't have to pack everything away at the end of each session.

She retrieved plates and some napkins before returning. "Why do you ask?"

"Because, if you do, I'd like to buy one."

Her laughter spilled out before she could stop it. "You're joking, right?"

"Not at all. I saw some paintings at one of the galleries today and they couldn't hold a candle to your work. It's something you should consider. Maybe build up a collection during the winter months when things are slow in your tour business."

His suggestion reflected her thoughts to a T. Something she found intriguing. Not to mention scary. "I'll keep that in mind. But right now—" her gaze drifted to the pizza box. "—all I can think about is what's in there."

"It does smell good, doesn't it?" He lifted the lid.

"That's not what you said the first time you saw me eating a pineapple pizza." Using a fork, she laid a slice on each plate.

"I tried it, didn't I?"

"After you accused me of trying to poison you."

He grinned. "Would you believe that I've ordered pineapple on my pizza ever since?"

Her heart stuttered as she licked the tangy sauce from her thumb. Then covered the reaction by turning her attention to the dogs. "You guys are hungry, too, aren't you?" Back in the kitchen, she filled their bowls and regained her composure.

"Well, one thing's for sure," she said, coming into the dining room. "Our son didn't inherit our affinity for above-average pizza."

"I like the way you said that."

She looked at him. "What?"

"*Our* son."

Heat crept into her cheeks. She cleared her throat. "What can I get you to drink? Water? Soda?"

"Water, please."

She escaped once again, filled two glasses with ice, then turned on the tap. "Austin said you guys played football today."

Returning to the table, she set a cup at each place and eased into the seat opposite Trent.

He nodded, his mouth full. "He's a good athlete."

"He loves sports. And he's not afraid to try new things." She savored her first bite. The sweet and salty flavors were like a colorful display of fireworks zinging around her mouth.

"Except pizza with pineapple."

"Yes, his adventurous streak wanes when it comes to food."

He cradled his half-eaten piece. "I hear you got your tour vehicle back."

She nodded. "Yesterday."

"That must be a relief."

"You have no idea." She washed down her next bite with a sip of water, surreptitiously watching the hunky man across from her. The barely there stubble that shadowed his square chin. Those long dark lashes her son had inherited. The subtle laugh lines that indicated he was a man who smiled often. Yeah, she was glad he was here. This was comfortable.

Maybe too comfortable.

Time to pull out some questions she'd had on her mind.

"What happened to your wife?" Okay, she probably could have been a little more tactful.

"Drunk driver."

Her hand flew to her mouth. "I…I didn't. I am so sorry."

"Don't be." He wiped his mouth with a paper napkin. "The driver was Lauren's boyfriend."

Her mouth fell open. Talk about out of left field.

He held up his crust. "Mind if I give this to the dogs?"

"Go ahead." His wife had a boyfriend?

He broke the crust into two pieces, tossed them to his attentive audience and dusted his hands off. "My marriage was a joke, Blakely. Not long after Lauren miscarried, she told me she didn't want to have children."

"But…you always wanted a family."

He reached for another slice. "Still do."

A breeze drifted through the window behind him, billowing the sheer curtain panel. Blakely didn't know what to say, so she focused on her pizza.

"At any rate, while I concentrated on my studies, Lauren was more interested in partying. I guess she thought being married to a doctor would be fun. That we'd be rich, attending one social event after the other."

"You hadn't even made it through medical school." She finished her first piece, including the crust, and started a second.

"Exactly. So…" He picked off a chunk of pineapple and popped it in his mouth. "She found new friends. And, thanks to your grandfather, I found God."

Her heart almost melted. "Really?"

He nodded. "All those talks he and I used to have took root. I came to realize I had a hole in my life that only God could fill."

She couldn't help smiling. "Granddad would have been happy to know that."

He leaned forward, his arms folded on the table. "Blakely, there's something I need to—"

Ding.

She pointed toward the office somewhere behind her. "I need to get that."

Trent managed to intercept the irascible Yorkie before he took off down the hall. "We'll be here when you get back."

After assisting a young couple with some restaurant recommendations, Blakely paused to collect her thoughts. Seemed Trent's life hadn't been as blissful as she'd imagined. Maybe he wasn't the man she'd made him out to be.

Back in the dining room, she found him studying photos of Austin, Jethro still tucked under his arm. He set the dog down on the carpet as she entered.

"Guess business is starting to pick up?"

"Praise God." She continued past him and reclaimed her

chair. "Things get a little lean sometimes, but He always provides."

Trent studied her a moment, as though he didn't believe her. Finally, he gestured to the now-closed pizza box. "Another slice? Or are you ready to move on to dessert?"

"Definitely more pizza."

He flipped the top open.

She grabbed a slice and scarfed it down as though she hadn't eaten the two before. "Guess I was hungrier than I thought."

He placed the last piece on her plate.

"Are you sure?"

"It's all yours."

She picked it up. "That'll teach me to have only a protein bar for lunch."

He folded his arms over his broad chest in a way that made his biceps look huge and glared down at her. "You do realize that's not healthy?"

"It's not like I make a habit of it."

He lifted a knowing brow.

"Much."

Chuckling, he again positioned himself across from her. "So when did you leave Denver?"

"About eight weeks after I returned." Her appetite evaporated as old memories surfaced. She set her pizza on her plate, picked at the bits of ham. "My stepmother was afraid my *condition,* as she called it, would tarnish my father's memory. Personally, I think she was more worried about her social status. How a pregnant stepdaughter might sully her reputation. She wanted to send me away somewhere to have the baby, and then put him up for adoption."

Trent's gaze narrowed.

"The whole idea scared me to death." She grabbed a napkin and concentrated on wiping her fingers. "Like I wasn't scared enough to begin with. I couldn't imagine giving up my baby. Not after losing my parents." She took a deep breath. "So, the night before I was supposed to leave, I got in my car and drove from Denver to Ouray. Gran and Granddad invited me to stay here and…" She glanced up. "I've never looked back."

Trent's Adam's apple bobbed, the muscle in his jaw twitching. After a silent moment, he rounded the table. Kneeling beside her, he took hold of her hands. "I can't tell you how sorry I am that you had to go through that alone, Blakely. If I had known…"

His gaze searched hers before drifting to her lips. Stayed there. Was he going to kiss her? Did he want to?

Her heart thundered as he leaned closer. It would be so easy…

She turned her head. "I'll take one of those truffles now."

After a slight hesitation, he stood and reached for the dark brown box. He opened it, set it in front of her. "Ladies first."

Spying a dark chocolate one, she grabbed it and took a bite, hoping to erase the memory of what had almost happened. What she'd wanted to happen. "How long are you planning to stay at the San Juan Inn?"

"Good question." He returned to his chair, clasped his hands atop the table. "It's getting a bit claustrophobic."

"I can imagine."

"I talked with a real estate agent about something temporary, an apartment or such, but apparently they're all occupied by college kids."

"They gotta live somewhere."

You have a vacant apartment.

No. She had a studio.

One you won't have any time to use this summer.

"Do you still lease the apartments over Adventures in Pink?"

"It's extra income. Yes." That voice inside her head was louder than ever now. *God, I do not want Trent living at Adventures in Pink. Not when I could lose my heart to him at any moment.* Still, if she wanted any peace…

She stole another truffle. A lavender one, hoping for calm. "As a matter of fact, I...have one apartment left. It's small, but—"

Those brown eyes went wide. "Small is fine."

Great. "Then, I guess it's ready whenever you are."

"You mean it?" The whimsical look on his face was priceless.

"Yeah."

"Perfect! Can I move in tomorrow?"

Chapter Thirteen

After church, Trent packed his things, loaded up his truck and checked out of his motel. Now he stared at the blue building on Seventh Avenue, amazed at what God was doing in his life.

Somehow God would restore his relationship with Blakely. Though how that could happen when Trent was in Albuquerque, he didn't have a clue.

Last night he'd again tried to tell her. Only to be interrupted—*again.* So, for now, he decided to let it go.

Inside Adventures in Pink, people milled about, waiting for the next tour.

"Yes. Your guide will make frequent stops, so there'll be plenty of opportunities for pictures." Blakely's voice came from somewhere behind the group. "Does everyone have water?"

A few held up bottles.

"Staying hydrated is very important at this altitude."

Trent jockeyed around a husky gentleman wearing a beige fedora. A few feet away, a gray-haired woman Trent assumed was the man's wife held up two T-shirts sporting hummingbirds and lettering that read Ouray, Colorado. "Should I get the purple or the pink?"

Preferring to remain inconspicuous until the crowd dissipated, Trent found an empty corner near the front window and waited. Funny. Not one canine had greeted him.

Then he noticed Ellie Mae sashaying across the blue-gray carpet, tail swishing from side to side. She nuzzled her head under his hand and sat on his feet. As Trent rubbed, her eyes closed, her tongue hung out one side of her mouth, and he was certain she smiled.

"Yes, sir. Thank you." The sound of Austin's voice captured Trent's attention.

He lifted his head and saw his son behind the ceramic-tile-topped snack bar, passing out bottled water to guests who'd opted for the last-minute purchase. The boy smiled at each person as they handed him their money.

Between Sunday school and worship service, Trent had heard all about Austin's sleepover with Zach. Although he had a sneaking suspicion there hadn't been much sleeping involved.

A man looking every bit the cowboy, from his boots to his Wranglers and straw Stetson, swept into the room, jerking Trent's attention back to the here and now. "Everyone on the one-thirty tour to Yankee Boy Basin, if you'd please make your way outside."

A mass exodus followed as the man Trent presumed was one of Blakely's guides grabbed a paperwork-topped clipboard. He spoke briefly with Blakely before joining the group outside.

Trent emerged from his hiding place as the door eased to a close.

"Dad!" Austin bounded around the snack counter. "I was wondering when you were gonna get here."

Across the room, behind a counter-high glass display case filled with geological finds, Blakely wore an apprehensive smile. Did she regret her decision to rent to him?

He continued toward the L-shaped desk. "Well, I'm here now and ready to move in."

"I've, uh, I've got your contract all ready." Blakely pulled out a file folder and set it on the counter. "It's a standard month-to-month lease."

She went over the highlights of the agreement, then handed him a pen.

Austin watched as he signed. "I can't believe you're going to be living here. This is so cool."

Blakely held out a set of keys. "Yours is the unit at the front of the building."

"The one with the balcony?" The best apartment of the three. That was a pleasant surprise.

"Yes."

He high-fived Austin. "I've got a view of Hayden Mountain."

"I'm sure you remember the way but, just in case, Austin, would you like to show Trent to his apartment?"

"Sure. Can I help him bring his stuff in, too?"

"That'll be fine." She returned the papers to the folder. "As long as it's okay with Trent."

"'Course it is. Not that I've got much."

"The larger key is to the door at the bottom of the stairs, and the smaller one is to your apartment. The outside door is to remain locked at all times."

"Got it." He turned to Austin. "Come on, buddy, let's get to work."

Austin bolted out the door ahead of Trent and toward the pickup. "This is so great. We can hang out all the time now."

"Hold up there, Austin. You may be on summer break, but I still have to work."

"Oh, yeah." His face scrunched in disappointment before brightening once again. "But when you're not, you'll be *right* here."

Trent ruffled Austin's hair, his heart light. "That's right, son. I'll be right here."

Wispy white clouds drifted aimlessly overhead, accentuating what was otherwise a lazy Sunday afternoon.

Trent handed Austin a duffel bag, then grabbed the rolling suitcase and a box containing books and files.

"I can carry more." The way the kid listed under the weight didn't bolster his claim.

"Sorry, this is all there is."

"Really?" The boy peered inside the vehicle as if he didn't believe him.

"Most of my stuff is still back in Albuquerque." Which meant a trip to Montrose might be in order. First, he'd better scope out the apartment to see exactly how furnished the place was.

On the east side of the building, near the garage bays, Austin unlocked the door to an inside stairwell. Trent followed his son, glancing down the narrow corridor at the top. Funny, he hadn't remembered it being quite so compact.

Austin shifted the bag to his other hand. "Maybe I can even sleep over sometimes." He shrugged. "That is, when you don't have to work."

"Great idea." Trent unlocked the door to their left. "Just us bachelors."

"Yeah, no girls allowed."

"Root beer and buffalo wings for—"

What will Austin think when he finds out you're leaving? That you chose work over him?

"Open the door, Dad."

"Sorry." Stepping inside, Trent let go a low whistle. "This doesn't look at all like I remembered."

An inviting shade of golden orange warmed his temporary abode. Scanning the small living room, he noted even the ceiling had been painted. A lighter yellow-gold that brightened the whole space.

This place had Blakely written all over it.

He set the box on what he thought was a wood floor, though, upon further inspection, turned out to be vinyl with the look of distressed oak. Smart move, given that college kids weren't traditionally known for their housekeeping skills.

While Austin roamed the apartment, flipping on lights, Trent crossed the small sitting area to a glass door that opened onto the balcony overlooking Seventh Avenue. Outside, two stackable lawn chairs flanked a small plastic table. With that view, he'd be spending a lot of time out there.

Turning back to the living room, he noted the brown leather-like sofa against the opposite wall and two bar stools lining a counter that opened to the small kitchen.

"The bedroom's back here."

He followed his son's voice down the short hall, past the bathroom, to a room barely big enough for the full-size bed, side table and chest of drawers that it housed. The bed was stripped bare, and Trent decided his trip to Montrose had better happen fast.

"Austin?" Blakely's voice trailed from the other room.

"Yeah?" The boy took off, and Trent followed.

Blakely stood in the doorway. "Zach's mom called. They're going to the hot springs and wanted to know if you'd like to go."

"Can I?"

Her gaze flicked to Trent then to Austin. "Sure. You probably won't be home until after dinner, so you'll need to take some money."

Trent reached for his wallet, feeling like a real dad. "How much do you need?"

The glare Blakely sent him indicated he was out of line. "We have a rule. I only give him enough for his meal. Any snacks are at Austin's expense. Right?"

Austin stood between the two of them, his gaze moving from Trent to Blakely. "Yes, ma'am."

She rested her hands on his shoulders. "He gets the profits from the drink sales downstairs."

"You don't say?"

"Even if I'm not there to sell it. I just have to keep it stocked."

"Sounds like the perfect job for someone your age." He pulled a five from his wallet, watching for Blakely's approval. "This okay?"

She nodded and Austin accepted the money.

"Thanks, Dad. Thanks, Mom." He took off down the stairs. "I gotta go get my swim trunks."

"Don't forget a towel," Blakely hollered after him as the lower door slammed close.

Trent returned the wallet to the back pocket of his jeans. "Thanks for keeping me on track. I'm still trying to get the hang of this parenting thing."

"You're doing fine."

"Thanks." He averted his gaze, trying not to think about his failed attempt to kiss her last night.

Still standing in the doorway, Blakely gestured inside the apartment with her fingers. "Do you mind if I—?"

"Not at all." He stepped aside, allowing her entry. "This place looks fantastic."

"Thank you. It was my winter project this year." She moved toward the kitchen. "I think I left something in here." She opened a cupboard and pulled out a small plastic box.

"What's that?"

"Some painting supplies." She shrugged as though it were nothing important. "Paints. Brushes. Palette."

"You mean you come up here to paint?"

"Occasionally. Not—not very often."

The way she tried to act like it was nothing had him suspecting it was something. Something that meant a lot to her. Something she'd given up for him.

With Austin gone and not much action at Adventures in Pink, Blakely was forced to find things to keep her mind off of Trent. She responded to email queries about trips and pricing. She refolded T-shirts that had been mussed. She even cleaned the bathroom.

Imagine. Trent Lockridge living right over her head. Seeing him every day.

What was she thinking?

She jumped at the telephone's tweedle.

"Adventures in Pink. This is Blakely. How may I help you?"

"Hey, this is Trent." The sound of his voice had her insides twisting. "I have a question. Do you think green would match the wall color in my apartment?"

She choked back a laugh. "Uh, depends on what shade of green."

He was silent so long she thought he'd hung up. "You still there?"

"Yeah. I'm just trying to decide the best way to describe this color."

"All right—" She leaned back in her chair as one of her favorite country songs drifted from the speakers across the room. "—try to think of foods or something in nature that looks like it. Like avocado."

"The inside or the outside?"

A burst of laughter spilled out. "Either one."

"Nope, not that."

"Okay, how about a lime, a pine tree or sage?"

"You mean like the seasoning?"

She dropped her head in her hand. Men. To most of them, green was green and blue was blue. "Let's see if I can make this easier. Is it a dark shade or a light shade?"

He paused. "More light than dark, but kind of in between."

"Does it lean more toward yellow, blue or gray?"

The rustle of paper or plastic filtered through the line. "Uh...you know that blouse you wore to church today?"

"Yes."

"It's about that color."

She wasn't sure whether to be shocked, flattered or annoyed that he'd paid such close attention to her attire. "That should match fine."

"Great. Thanks, Blakely."

Her curiosity piqued as she hung up the cordless handset. At least she finally had a tenant who cared about his surroundings.

An hour later, Trent's pickup pulled into a parking space in front of the building. Blakely wouldn't have noticed had he not parked right in front of the door. At least, that's what she told herself.

He skirted around to the passenger side, opened the door and stooped inside. When he emerged, several plastic bags dangled from one hand. With the other, he tossed the door closed before reaching into the bed of the truck to grab a medium-size box bearing an image of a flat-panel TV. Then he disappeared around the side of the building.

Tucking her curiosity aside, Blakely checked email, happy to find another inquiry. As she typed her response, Trent appeared in her periphery. She didn't want to watch him, yet something compelled her. Still more bags, what looked like a bedspread or comforter and—she laughed—a green lampshade.

He paused outside the screen door and looked right at her. "Something funny in there?"

She craned her neck as though she couldn't quite see him. "I'm sorry. Were you talking to me?"

Grinning, he walked away.

She cringed and turned back to the computer.

Ellie Mae glanced up at her from beneath the counter.

"What?"

The dog lifted her brow, brown eyes drooping.

"I was minding my own business. He just…got in the way. That's all."

Seemingly unconvinced, the canine sighed before dropping her head atop her paws.

Blakely scowled. "You should've stayed home with Jethro."

If Trent returned again, she didn't notice. Instead, she updated trail conditions on the company's website until the screen door creaked open.

She turned to find Trent on the other side of the cash register, smiling at her. Rarely had a plain white T-shirt looked so good.

"I need a favor."

"O-kay."

"I bought one of those put-it-together-yourself television stands. The box is kind of heavy. Do you suppose I could get you to hold open the door to the stairwell for me?"

"Sure." She grabbed the cordless phone, shoved it in the side pocket of her cargo shorts and followed him out the door.

He lifted the box from the back of his truck and hoisted it onto his shoulder, his muscles bulging.

"What about that coffeemaker? Does it go up, too?"

He glanced back. "How could I forget that? Yes, please. If you don't mind."

She snatched the box before scurrying to open the side door. "You sure you don't need any help with that?" She continued behind him, up the stairs.

"Why? Do I look like I need help?" The smile in his voice was like sweet torture.

"Not really."

He shoved open the door to his apartment and set the box in the middle of the living room before turning to her. "But thanks for asking."

Her stomach flip-flopped.

"Where would you like this?" She held out the coffeemaker.

"I'll take it." His hand brushed hers, setting a tingling wave of excitement dancing up her arm.

She rubbed the goose bumps away, surveying his purchases. The green stripes in the brown comforter matched the lampshade to a tee. "That'll look great with the wall color."

"I hoped it would." He set the box on the pass-through between the kitchen and sitting area. "And then I thought the green shade would look good on the lamp on the nightstand."

"I'm impressed." She met his gaze. "Most of my tenants don't put so much thought into their surroundings."

Reaching over, he tucked a wayward hair behind her ear, the heat of his finger searing her skin. "I bet there are a lot of things around here they don't appreciate."

Chapter Fourteen

Blakely had less than an hour before the next round of tours, so if she didn't eat now, she might not get to at all. Dropping the white paper bag on the Adventures in Pink snack bar, she continued to the garage and poked her head around the storm door.

"Lunch is here."

"All right." Austin wheeled from under Trent's pickup, still holding the droplight. "I'm starving." He'd spent the morning helping change the oil and had dark greasy splotches all over his face.

Trent rolled into view, looking every bit as dirty as her son. Except, on him, the look was incredibly attractive. "Perfect timing. We just finished." His black T-shirt was taut across his massive chest, the color lending a smoldering appearance to his dark eyes.

She cleared her throat. "Well, from where I stand, it looks like it's going to take you guys a while to get cleaned up so you'd better hop to it. Especially you, young man." She caught her son's eye. "You can't sell drinks looking like that."

"Yes, ma'am." Austin set the droplight on the workbench against the wall.

Closing the door, she allowed her gaze to linger on Trent. She kind of liked having him around. He was good for Austin.

What about you?

She took a deep breath. From all appearances, Trent was the whole package. But appearances could be deceiving, and that made her reluctant to act on her feelings. Feelings that seemed to be getting stronger every day.

Turning her back on the guys, she climbed the handful of steps and unpacked their sandwiches from the deli. A grilled cheese for Austin, a southwest turkey for Trent and her favorite, the turkey cranberry on an asiago bagel.

In the week since Trent had moved in, life hadn't changed as much as she'd feared. He was gone most of the day, arriving home an hour or so before closing time. But he always came in to ask about her day and if there was anything he could do to help her out.

Austin, however, usually met his father the moment he stepped out of his truck and they'd spend a couple hours playing or talking, simply getting to know one another.

She smiled, shaking her head. Trent looked so weary some nights, yet he always had time and a smile for Austin. A trait she found endearing.

Opening a small bag of potato chips, she popped one in her mouth. All in all, this had been a stellar week. She'd hired a new guide, tours were up and Ross Chapman hadn't dropped by once. Maybe the guy had given up.

Now, if only she were as adept on the administrative side of things, life would be perfect. As it was, spreadsheets and anything having to do with taxes and payroll were the bane of her existence. Her office desk had so many piles, she wouldn't see the beautiful oak finish until December.

"What does your mom have to say about this?" Trent's voice was followed by the slamming of the door.

Austin rounded the corner first, looking freshly scrubbed and wearing a clean shirt. "She said it was okay."

"What did I say was okay?" She handed Austin his sandwich and a bag of Cheetos.

"To take Dad Jeeping on Father's Day."

"Ah." She passed Trent his lunch before grabbing her own. "Yes, Austin said he wanted to do something nice for your first Father's Day. And, since he'd mentioned earlier that you liked Jeeping, we thought you might enjoy a day in the mountains."

His slow smile had her scurrying back to the reception desk to eat. "That sounds amazing. A day in the mountains with my two favorite people." The look he sent her made it impossible to think.

Luckily, Austin picked up the conversation from there, telling Trent all the things he wanted to show him, while Blakely concentrated on her sandwich.

"Did you restock the refrigerator, Austin?" Finished, she balled the paper wrapping and tossed it in the wastebasket under the counter.

"With water and sodas." Austin finally took a bite of his sandwich. Too much chattering, not enough eating.

"Good deal." A strange odor touched her nostrils as she came around the desk. "Do you smell something?"

A few feet away, Trent sniffed. "Yeah. Smells like—"

"Fire!" Seeing the smoke-filled garage, Blakely practically threw herself down the handful of steps.

Trent and Austin were right behind her.

On the other side of the glass door, smoke billowed through the shop. Her heart pounded as she blew through the door. Fumes stung her eyes and burned her throat.

She reached for the fire extinguisher hanging on the wall beside the door, then whirled toward Trent. "Get your truck out of here. Austin! Outside!"

"But, Mom!"

"Go!"

Trent tossed the boy into the truck ahead of him. Slammed the vehicle into Reverse.

Coughing, she aimed the extinguisher at a pile of rags. What few flames there were quickly succumbed to the white foam. Still, she wasn't about to take any chances.

The red extinguisher hissed as she fingered the trigger again, its foamy contents coating tools, tires and more. She choked.

Trent jerked the extinguisher from her hands. "Go!" He shoved her toward the door.

The now-white smoke followed her into the alley, the breeze quickly whisking it away.

Blakely gasped for air. Coughed. Gasped again as Trent emerged from the garage.

"That was scary." Austin's eyes were as big as hubcaps.

"Yes, it was." Blakely hugged him close.

"The important thing is that we're all safe." Trent coughed.

She couldn't disagree there.

Out of the corner of her eye, she saw people gathering near the corner of the building. Heard their murmurs. Guests for the one-thirty tour.

Oh, no.

"Just a little mishap, folks." Ross Chapman herded them toward the front door. "Nothing to worry about." He turned to Blakely. "If you need to deal with things, though, Mountain View Tours would be happy to cover for you."

Trent glared at Ross. "Don't worry, Chapman. We've got things covered."

Ross started to walk away, then turned, flashing her guests a dazzling smile. "If any of you folks feel uncomfortable, come on up to Mountain View Tours. We'll take good care of you."

His parting words settled in the pit of Blakely's stomach. Luckily, not one guest took him up on his offer. And although she'd calmly recited her spiel to her guests and sent them on their way with the guide, inside she was wound up tighter than a pair of Nicole Chapman's jeans.

Her breathing intensified. The garage was filled with petroleum products. There could have been an explosion. Austin. The apartments. People could have been killed.

Gasping for air, she dropped into her chair. How could this happen?

She tried to catch her breath but couldn't.

"Blakely?" Trent stepped in front of her.

"I—I can't...breathe."

"You're hyperventilating." He rubbed her shoulders. "Calm down. Concentrate on your breathing."

"I...can't." She felt like a Jeep had been dropped on her chest.

His hands left her. Paper crinkled.

"Here." He shoved the paper bag from lunch into her hands. "Hold this over your nose and mouth and try to breathe normally."

He stroked her back and, with a great deal of effort, she followed his instruction. "Where's...where's Austin?"

"I sent him home. I had a feeling you might crash and burn once the tour left. Figured you wouldn't want him to see."

Since when did he know her so well?

Her air intake finally evened out and she removed the bag. "Thank you."

"You're welcome." Concern puckered his brow as he continued to watch her.

What would she have done without him?

Deciding some things were better left unexplored, she stood and returned the bag to the trash. "Have you had a chance to investigate? See what happened out there?" She poked a thumb toward the shop.

"Not yet."

"Shall we then?" She led the way into the garage. Though the air had cleared, the unmistakable smell of smoke still lingered.

Trent's gaze scanned the plethora of tires and chemicals. "Good thing we caught it early. If this had gotten out of control—"

She held up a hand. "Do you want me to start hyperventilating again?"

One corner of his mouth lifted. "Sorry."

They stopped beside the partially burned pile of oily rags and knelt for a better look. The workbench and everything around them was covered in white film. Aside from that, things looked pretty much unscathed.

"Uh-oh." Frustration lined Trent's face as he reached into the center of the pile and picked up what had once been the droplight. "How could I have been so careless?"

"You?"

He held up the light. "This was my fault. I should have made sure Austin took care of this properly." He raked his free hand through his hair. Groaned. "From the looks of things—" he glanced at the rags "—it was still on."

While Blakely tried to follow his train of thought, she knew he was mistaken. "No. Austin did take care of it. I saw him."

Trent's eyes went wide. "You did?"

"Yes. He laid it on the workbench." She pointed just above their heads.

Trent looked as dumbfounded as she felt. "So how did it—?"

Their gazes collided.

Blakely felt the blood drain from her face. "Are you thinking what I'm thinking?"

"That it could have fallen?"

"Or somebody moved it." Blakely pushed to her feet.

Trent did, too, all the while eyeing her suspiciously. "I'm not following you."

"How was it that Ross just happened to be passing by?"

"Blakely, I appreciate you trying to let me off the hook, but do you really think Ross would do something like this?"

"I hope not." But seeing how the guy didn't like the word no, she wasn't about to put anything past him.

* * *

"There's a package for you, Dr. Lockridge."

Over the gray Formica counter, Trent eyed the bulky express envelope in the receptionist's hand. "Would you mind holding on to that for me, Judy, until I'm finished with my next patient?"

"Sure thing, doctor." She set it aside as he grabbed a file folder and started down the hallway at the clinic.

The day he and Scott had plotted and planned for years had finally arrived. He remembered the first time they walked into the beige stucco office building. They'd looked at dozens of buildings, but that one just felt right.

Until now.

One well-baby check, an ear infection and a bee sting later, he retrieved the package from the front desk.

For the umpteenth time, his phone vibrated in his pocket. And for the umpteenth time, Scott's name appeared on the screen.

"Hey, guy." Trent slipped into the clinic's small break room at the back of the building, pleased to find it empty.

"Finally," said Scott. "I was beginning to think you were avoiding me."

He glanced at the round wall clock. Eleven-fifteen. "I may not be in Albuquerque, but I still have to work, you know."

"Did you get the papers?"

"I'm holding them in my hand." He thumped the package against his thigh.

"You know you have to have them notarized, right?"

His friend was the driving force propelling their dream into reality. Without Scott's vision and take-charge attitude, Trent never would have been able to pull this off.

And Scott can't do this alone.

He slumped against the wall. "I do."

"Once the title company gets them back, I can pick up the

keys and we can really get this ball rolling. Rebecca settled on gold, by the way."

"Gold?"

"For the walls. Golden Garden she called it. I don't know— still looks beige to me."

Trent laughed, recalling his conversation with Blakely when he was picking out stuff for his apartment. "Well, whatever it is, I have no doubt Rebecca will do a fine job."

"So…when are you going to sign those papers?"

He smiled at one of the nurses who came to refresh her coffee. "I have one more patient before lunch. Maybe I can break away—"

"I knew you wouldn't let me down, buddy."

His heart felt like an anvil. "Never."

"We've both got a lot riding on this. The sooner we finish these renovations, the sooner we can start helping folks."

He checked the clock again. "Speaking of which, I need to get to my next patient."

When Trent finally took a seat at the bank's shiny desk, the midday sun was beating down on the jagged Sawtooth Range.

It wasn't like he was turning his back on Austin, right? Six hours wasn't so bad. Trent could make the drive once a month. At least that was his plan.

Still, he wanted so much more—ball games, homework, those spontaneous visits to the ice cream parlor…Blakely.

He picked up the pen and scrawled his signature wherever the sticky yellow arrows pointed, then left before he could change his mind.

Too bad his head and his heart were no longer on the same page.

Chapter Fifteen

Trent couldn't think of any place he'd rather spend his first Father's Day than riding through the mountains with the boy who could be his clone laughing in the backseat.

Praise You, Lord.

The sun shone brightly as Blakely drove the pink Jeep over the winding, craggy roads. More than once they had to stop for what she referred to as road maintenance, removing large rocks or other debris from their path.

Above the timberline, lingering snow clung to mountainsides, while below the runoff cut a swath through pine-tree-carpeted slopes.

"How high are we?" Holding on to the roll bar, he glanced at Blakely.

She eyed Austin in the rearview mirror. "Would you like to guess?"

The boy studied their surroundings. "Ten thousand feet?"

"Very good." Pride was evident in his mother's smile.

"How much farther?" Trent had heard Austin talk about this place for the past week, but he didn't have a clue as to its whereabouts.

Sporting a mischievous smile, Blakely whipped the vehicle

off of the main road and onto a narrow trail. "You're worse than a ten-year-old."

Austin grinned.

Up ahead, a stream surged over rocks, veering left and right, before drifting along a gentle straightaway. Budding wildflowers nestled among its stony banks, beauty among the chaos.

Trent braced himself, fearing Blakely would plow through this stream the way she had that one a few weeks ago. Instead, she came to a stop before reaching the water.

Austin launched himself over the edge of the Jeep. "You gotta come see this, Dad. Mom and I were up here last year, and we found this old mine. It's not even boarded up like most of them."

"That sounds great, but we still need to be careful." Trent shut his door behind him, eyeing the thinning spread of towering pines that paved the way toward snowcapped peaks. "There's a reason most of them are off-limits."

"I know."

Reveling in the crisp mountain air, he met Blakely at the back of the Jeep and grabbed the picnic basket while she tucked an old quilt over her arm. "Where to?"

"How about over there?" She pointed to a level spot a few feet from the water's edge.

Following her, watching Austin balance across a log, his smile bright as the sun, Trent felt like the luckiest guy in the world. This was his dream. Family. A mom, a dad and their son enjoying a Sunday afternoon together. Nothing could be better.

Except maybe to have Blakely as his wife.

But his decision to follow his head ensured that wouldn't happen.

He shook away the remorse. Nothing was going to ruin this day.

"Come on, Dad."

He eyed Blakely. "Are you coming?"

She hugged the quilt to her chest. "I'll catch up."

Trent followed his son over boulders and around trees.

"The mine shafts look kinda small, but inside they could be *huge*." Austin flung his arms through the air. "The miners would tunnel up and down and across. Sometimes there'd be big caves. They'd even keep their mules inside."

Trent ducked under a low branch. "And all with nothing more than candles to light their way, right?"

"Yeah." Austin dodged around a mud puddle. "One guy would hold this big steel rod—" he held his hands about two feet apart "—and the guy with the hammer would aim for the shine. That's what they called the spot where the candle on his helmet would reflect off the head of the spike. Then the guy holding the rod would give it a turn and wait for the next hit, until they had it deep enough to shove in a stick of dynamite."

"Guess you'd better trust the guy doing the swinging."

Austin laughed. "Yeah."

Winded, Trent struggled to keep up with his energetic son. "How do you know so much about mining? Did they teach you in school?"

The boy shrugged. "A little. I just like it. They have this really cool exhibit in the basement of the museum. You can learn all kinds of stuff about mining. And Mr. Jenkins is there sometimes. He used to be a miner. Whenever he talks, I just listen."

As they rounded a mound of crushed rock, the mine shaft came into view. About the size of a large door, the rectangular opening cut a couple dozen feet into the side of the mountain. Ice clung to the entrance, though some had broken free, crashing to the floor in a slushy mess.

Austin picked his way closer. "Cool, isn't it?"

Running a hand along the rough edges of the rock, Trent eased inside far enough to know he shouldn't risk going any farther. He peered into the utter blackness, realizing someone had blasted this hole out of the face of the mountain. Something he found eerily fascinating.

"And then over here…" Austin pushed the limb of a pine tree out of his way and continued farther into the woods.

Trent took one last perusal of the shaft, then followed Austin's trail through a thick cluster of pines. At a small outcropping, Austin waited. When he saw Trent, he pointed below to the remnants of an old stamping mill. No telling how many years the thing had been there, surviving countless winters and avalanches.

"I think the guys who had that mine brought the ore down here for stamping." Austin looked up at Trent, excitement gleaming in his big brown eyes. "That's how they got the gold out of the ore. These big hammers would go up and down—" he demonstrated with his fists "—smashing the rocks."

"Yes, Ouray didn't used to be the quiet little town you see now."

Turning, he couldn't help smiling at Blakely. "How so?"

"There were some pretty large operations in the area. Camp Bird, for instance." She pointed in the distance. "They had a huge stamping mill that ran 24/7. All that noise reverberated through the canyons right down into town."

"I never thought about that before, but I guess you're right." He tried to imagine what life must have been like for the miners. People from all walks of life, hoping to strike it rich, had endured hardships way beyond his urban comprehension. "I might have to check out the Ouray Museum."

"Lunch is ready, if you guys are hungry." She nodded in the direction of the Jeep.

"Good. I'm starving." As if someone had flipped a switch, Austin took off.

Blakely laughed, a sound Trent would never tire of hearing. "Growing boys."

"Has he always been this curious?"

"Oh, yeah. There's not a lot that gets past him." Her sweet smile filled him with gratitude.

He reached for her hand. Tugged her close. "Thank you,

Blakely, for making my first Father's Day one I'll always remember."

To his surprise, her slender fingers closed around his. She met his gaze.

Easy. Natural.

He studied the curve of her face, her delicate nose, her sweet lips.

Inching closer, he lowered his head and kissed her gently. She tasted of strawberries and cream.

When she didn't resist, he wound his free arm around her waist, pulled her against him.

Her featherlight touch trailed over his shoulders, up his neck, caressed his hair. Her heart pounded against him, keeping rhythm with his own.

Hope sprang forth within him. She was everything he'd ever wanted. Home. Hearth. Family. Love.

Her body stiffened. She took a giant step back, her breathing ragged. The past and the present warred behind those blue eyes. The undeniable attraction that lay between them.

"We'd best get back."

Blakely paused for a breather, taking in the majestic view of the Amphitheater from Portland Trail. She hoped the hike might help clear her mind, but thoughts of Trent's kiss were still as fresh as the moment it happened—two days ago.

Seemed like her head and heart were in a constant battle. When she was with Trent, it all seemed so right. But away from him, her common sense presented some strong evidence to the contrary.

"If Ross Chapman knows what's good for him, he'd better stay away." Taryn uncapped her water bottle and took a drink. "Otherwise he'll have to deal with me"

Blakely almost spewed her water. "Since when did you become my protector?"

"Hey, we're in this together, chickie."

A grosbeak flitted from one pine branch to the next, its song welcoming the new day.

"And I'm sure Ross will be shaking in his boots."

"Well, he should." Taryn clipped her bottle onto the carabiner hanging from her belt and began their descent. "So how was your outing with Trent?"

"He kissed me." Something she wouldn't mind repeating.

"Whoa-ho-ho, Blakes. Did you kiss him back?"

"Yes, but—"

"Did you like it?"

"Yes, but—"

"Sounds like everybody's on the same page." Her friend dodged around a cedar. "So what's the problem?"

"The problem, if you would be so kind as to let me speak, is I liked them eleven years ago, too. You remember, right before he ripped the heart out of my chest and tossed it off Mt. Sneffels."

"Blakely, Blakely, Blakely." Taryn shook her head. "Do you recall our old buddy, King David?"

Gravel crunched underfoot as they ventured a steep slope.

"Sure. He was a man after God's own heart."

"And how many times did he mess up?"

"Let's see.... Adulterer, murderer—"

"Exactly! And when he repented of his sins, God forgave him."

She eyed her friend, the wind rustling through the trees. "I know where you're going with this."

"Did Trent have a personal relationship with Jesus Christ all those years ago?"

She shook her head.

"But he does now, right?"

From what she'd seen, he was just the kind of godly man she'd always wanted.

She kicked at a rock. "I guess."

"Blakes, what happens when we ask God to forgive our sins?"

"He throws them as far as the east is from the west."

Taryn stopped and Blakely almost ran into her. "If God forgave Trent, who are you not to?"

"Even if I forgive him, that doesn't mean I want a relationship with him. Too much water under the bridge." At least that was the argument her head presented.

"Blakes…" She laid a hand on Blakely's arm. "I'm afraid you haven't even made it to the bridge. Fear has you stuck upstream, clinging to the past. A past that's preventing you from looking at the possibility of a future. With Trent or anyone else."

Ouch!

She moved around Taryn to continue her trek. "You do realize this is starting to turn into a love/hate relationship."

"I know." Taryn plodded along behind her. "You love me, but you hate my advice because it steps all over those pretty little pink-painted toes of yours?"

"Ah, the lady is smarter than she looks."

Taryn nudged her from behind.

Rounding onto a nice straightaway, Blakely said, "Race you to the finish."

With any luck, the distraction would derail the conversation. She moved as quickly as the terrain would allow, whisking past brush and small boulders, her steps almost silent against a carpet of pine needles.

Her side ached. Sweat trailed down her back. She slowed her pace to a walk.

Taryn matched her steps, her breathing as labored as Blakely's. "I know. You want me. To drop this. And I will. Just as soon…as I have my say." She stopped Blakely with a hand to her shoulder. Drew in a deep breath. "I can't help feeling… that God's up to something here."

Blakely had entertained that very thought on more than

one occasion. But if God was at work, why wasn't He letting her know?

Maybe you're so busy waging your own battles, you forgot to check in with Him.

"All I'm saying is keep an open mind, Blakes. Or, as your grandmother says, you just might miss a blessing."

Chapter Sixteen

"Hi, Mr. Davis. This is Blakely Daniels with Adventures in Pink, in Ouray." Reaching across the front desk, she grabbed her calendar. "Hey, I wanted to let you know that I've mailed your contract for this year's tour and—"

"I'm sorry, young lady. We've decided to go with Mountain View Tours this year."

"Oh." She blinked, her heart lodging somewhere in the vicinity of her throat. The Active Life Seniors group out of Grand Junction had been coming to them for the past seven years. She'd just assumed...

"A fellow contacted us last month with a deal that was too good for folks on a fixed income to turn down."

She knew exactly who that fellow was. "You know, Mountain View Tours doesn't offer the customized tours Active Life Seniors enjoy with Adventures in Pink—"

"We've already signed the contract."

She had to dig deep for an air of professionalism to hide her disappointment. "I see. Well, then you can disregard our contract. We thank you for your business and hope we can serve you again in the future."

Hanging up the phone, she felt like she'd been punched in the stomach. Sucker punched by Ross Chapman.

She slumped back in her chair. This was her fault. She should have contacted the seniors group sooner instead of shoving them to the back burner while she tried to juggle everything else.

She'd even figured the income into her budget. Stupid. Now she'd have to find a way to make it up.

Maybe Ross was right. What did she know about running a business?

Turning to the computer at the front desk, she palmed the mouse and glanced out the window. This morning's tour to Yankee Boy was back and the six smiling faces soothed her wounded pride.

The youngest of the three couples ambled up the street, hand in hand, while the other two headed inside ahead of their guide. Blakely went to meet them.

"How was your tour?" She addressed them corporately, remembering the two men and two women were traveling together.

"Incredible!" Mrs. Barkus's once neatly coifed hair now sported a windblown look. "No wonder they call Ouray the Switzerland of America."

"That's for sure," added her always-smiling husband. "This place is amazing. This town is amazing."

"We like to think so."

Mrs. Hillard leaned against the counter. "We'd never even heard of it until we pulled in yesterday."

Her husband, a bald man with a British accent, nodded. "That's right. But it didn't take long to realize we'd found something special."

"We like to hear that." Blakely plucked a visitor's guide from the stack on the counter. "If you have a chance you should stop by the museum or take a walking tour around town." She flipped to the page that showed all of the homes on the tour. "Did you know that two thirds of Ouray's original Victorian structures are still in use?"

Mrs. Barkus eyed the descriptions of more than two dozen homes. "Oh, let's do that after lunch."

"Count me in." Mrs. Hillard pointed to a picture of the Western Hotel. "That's right next door, isn't it?"

"Yes, it is. And it's definitely a must-see."

"Now before you women get ahead of yourselves," said Mr. Hillard, "don't forget we wanted to book a full-day tour for tomorrow."

Blakely sent her new guide an appreciative smile. "Well then, let's get you set up." She shared the available options with the group, knowing a couple of the passes were still closed.

"Ghost towns?" Mr. Barkus quirked a brow.

"It's one of our most popular tours. You'll see the Red Mountain Mining District and Animas Forks, along with some of the most stunning views in the area."

"Not to mention lunch in Silverton," her guide added.

"Can we get Rodney as our driver again?" Mrs. Hillard glanced at her guide.

Ah, the new guy was already getting requests. A good sign.

"I believe we can work that out."

She sent up a prayer of thanksgiving as the quartet filed out of the office in search of some lunch. God would provide.

"Speaking of lunch..." Rodney tucked his clipboard in the wall rack. A teacher at the high school, he decided he might as well get paid for what he did all summer anyway. "I think I'll grab some, too. Would you like me to bring you anything?"

"No, I'm good. But thanks." Returning to the computer, she tapped the space bar to bring up the screen. Nothing but black.

"We'll see you in a few, then."

"Uh-huh." Trying to temper her frustration, she wiggled the mouse. Clicked. Double clicked. Still nothing.

Cantankerous thing must have frozen again.

Reaching under the counter, she pushed the button on the system unit to shut it down, then rebooted it as the door to the garage opened.

Still black. Only this time a series of skulls with crossbones dotted the screen. A wave of panic rolled over her.

"That can't be good." Dan sidled beside her.

"How can this be? I just updated our security stuff."

Dan raised his hands in the air. "Hey, I know nothing about computers, so don't ask me."

"What am I supposed to do without my computer? And all my files?"

"Don't you back it up?"

"Yes, but…" Grabbing her phone, she did an internet search for viruses. "It says I need to install anti-malware."

"I'll take your word for it."

That meant a trip to Montrose and who knows how many hours to get things up and running normally again. She did not want to deal with this now.

"Do you think Lisa would be willing to come in for an hour or so while I run to the store?"

"Probably. So long as you don't mind Alyssa tagging along."

"Of course not." She picked up the phone, but he pulled it from her hand.

"Just go."

Since kissing Blakely that day on the mountain, Trent found himself thinking about her more and more. About the three of them. Together. As a family.

But how could he even think about forging a relationship with Blakely when he wasn't being completely honest with her?

Pulling into a parking spot in front of Adventures in Pink, he saw she was still inside. He had to tell her.

He exited his truck, continued up the front steps and opened the door. "You're here awfully late."

Blakely's dejected gaze slid from the computer screen.

"Uh-oh. What's—" Before he could ask, she burst into tears.

"Blakely?" He kept his voice gentle as he moved around the desk. If this had anything to do with Ross Chapman...

She buried her face in her hands as he came alongside her. "I'm no good at this." She sobbed. "Granddad was wrong. I can't run this place."

He wanted to take her into his arms and erase any trace of whatever it was that had her so upset. "Now, what makes you say that?" He settled for caressing her back, her hair.

"This is the worst day ever." Through her weeping, she listed the problems she encountered. "None of this stuff ever happened when Granddad was here."

"Probably because he had you here to help him."

"Some help. More like destroyer."

He urged her hands from her face. Her cheeks were red, splotchy. But she still looked beautiful to him.

He handed her a couple tissues from the box on the counter. "Do you mind if I flip the closed sign? Shut the door?"

"Go ahead. I wouldn't—" she hiccupped "—want customers seeing me like this anyway."

When he returned, he pulled a stool alongside her and took hold of her hands, brushing his thumbs over her knuckles. Anything that might comfort her. "Blakely, from what your grandmother has told me, you and Bill were a pretty good team. Your marketing ideas breathed life into a sleepy little business. You encouraged him as much as he encouraged you."

She bit her quivering bottom lip.

"But the team's been cut to one player." He touched her cheek. "So you need to cut yourself a little slack."

"But Granddad did it all by himself." She sniffed.

"Over the course of thirty-five years. How long have you been running things? Six, seven months?"

"Eight."

He threw both hands in the air. "Oh, well. My mistake. You should have things down by now, then."

Her laughter was like the sweetest music he'd ever heard.

"We all have our strengths, Blakely. Your knowledge of and passion for these mountains run deep."

She shredded one of the tissues into her lap. "But it takes me two days to do payroll. And I have less than ten employees."

"Then maybe you should consider hiring someone to do those things you're not so adept at, allowing you to concentrate on the things you are."

"I don't know if I can afford another employee."

Ross's claim that she was losing business popped into his brain.

"You'd only need somebody part-time. Maybe a couple days a week." He tipped his head to look at her. "And by freeing yourself to focus on those things you are good at, your bottom line should improve."

She looked up at him, her gaze warm, tender...trusting.

"In the meantime, if you need some help or a tutorial, I happen to be good with numbers. Not to mention a whiz at spreadsheets."

"But you're a doctor." She sat up straight, stretched.

"Yes, but I love numbers, too. If I hadn't wanted to be a doctor so badly, I probably would have been an accountant."

"I don't think I ever knew that about you." She stood and crossed to the snack bar. "Care for one?" She held up a bottle of water.

"Sure." He met her halfway. "Have you eaten?"

"No. And I'm starving."

"Now you sound like Austin." He grinned. "What do you say I order us up a ham, pineapple and black olive pizza? I'll buy, you fly."

She gestured to the computer. "But what about—"

"I'll take care of the computer. You need a break."

"Thank you." She toyed with the label on the bottle. "You know, I'm not usually a crier. And here you've had to put up with my blubbering twice."

Using his finger, he tilted her chin up, forcing her to look at him. "Guess that makes me special, then."

Her cheeks turned pink. Not the upset splotches like before, but an irresistible blush. "Yeah, you kind of are."

Chapter Seventeen

In the kitchen of the community center, Blakely yawned and added ten more pancakes to the warming tray. "You know, Taryn, I wouldn't flip pancakes at 6:00 a.m. for just anyone." No matter how incredible they smelled.

"But you do it so well." Her friend hovered over the worktable, pouring syrup from a commercial-size container into smaller glass dispensers.

"This coming from the baker extraordinaire? You could probably handle this fund-raiser with one hand tied behind your back."

"Bake sale? Maybe." Taryn screwed on the handled lids. "Pancake breakfast? No."

Blakely laughed and took another sip of her coffee. The Mountain Rescue Team's annual Fourth of July breakfast was their biggest fund-raiser of the year. Composed of volunteers like Taryn, the team was available 24/7 for search and rescue operations in the surrounding mountain communities. All without charge. Blakely might like to razz her friend, but she wouldn't miss the opportunity to help.

"Where's Austin?"

"He's helping the guys set up." She nodded in the direction

of the main room as she ladled more batter onto the griddle. "Did I tell you I booked a new group?"

"No." Taryn licked syrup from her fingers before washing her hands.

"A group of doctors from Albuquerque is doing a retreat/ motivational thing in the area later this month. And get this— there are twice as many people as the seniors group, so they've booked tours for two days."

"That's great." Taryn turned off the water and reached for a paper towel. She leaned against the counter. "I am curious, though. Doctors? Albuquerque?"

"Yes, Trent had something to do with it. They were going to be in Telluride anyway. He simply suggested a Jeep tour."

"I bet he did more than suggest. I'm sure he completely sold you. Of course, it's totally worth it. For you and your guests." She pointed to the griddle. "Sounds like the good doctor is pretty handy to have around."

Blakely flipped the bubble-topped cakes. Trent had tackled more fix-it projects in both her building and the motel than she and Gran managed in a year. Not to mention, she now had a basic understanding of spreadsheets.

"I'm getting used to the situation." Used to having him show up at just the right time, always knowing exactly what to say to make her feel better.

"Situation, huh?" Taryn grabbed the tray of syrup containers and started toward the door. "And what exactly might that be?"

"Not what you're thinking." She sent her friend a knowing glance. "Yet."

"We have a line outside." Matt Stephens, another of Ouray's mountain guides, burst into the kitchen, nearly hitting Taryn with the swinging door.

"Matthew!" she glared.

"My bad." He took the tray from her. "We need to be ready to roll in ten."

"These two trays are full—" Blakely gestured to the large foil-covered buffet pans on the counter "—and the third will be shortly."

"Perfect." He pushed through the door. "Order up!"

Eric Hoffman, the town's lone plumber, and Nolan Dickerson, owner of Ouray's only year-round T-shirt shop, filed into the kitchen. Taryn handed each of them a pan as Blakely topped off the next and started another round.

"Sausage?" Nolan's wife, Susan, entered as the men left.

"In the oven." Taryn pointed, pulling crocks of individual butter packets and coffee creamer from the refrigerator. "Are the plates and utensils already out there?"

Susan snagged a couple of pot holders from a drawer and opened the oven. "Yes."

"I can carry something." Austin looked so cute in his pink Adventures in Pink T-shirt.

"Here you go." Taryn passed him the tubs. He tucked one in the crook of each arm, then used his body to hold the door open for Susan.

The noise from the main room grew louder, indicating they were open for business.

"Looks like we're on." Taryn paused beside Blakely, and tilted her head, her expression thoughtful. "I know what it's like to be betrayed, Blakes. But trust is a choice. I may not have found a man worthy of mine yet." She shrugged. "But I sure don't want to miss it when he does come along."

Batch after countless batch, Taryn's words echoed through Blakely's mind even after she relinquished her duties to high-tail it over to Adventures in Pink. Trent was supposed to decorate one of the tour trucks for the parade. Something that must have taken him longer than he expected because he never made it in for pancakes.

Rounding the corner onto Seventh Avenue, she stopped dead in her tracks. The tour truck was bare. And Trent's pickup was nowhere in sight.

She tugged her cell phone from her back pocket. No calls. No texts.

Great. Miss Teen Colorado was due any minute.

She snagged the untouched box of decorations off of the porch. "Austin, let's put the bunting along the sides, then we'll add some more streamers to the rails." Blakely attached a red banner to the back of the truck identifying their rider, Jenna Hightower, as Miss Teen Colorado.

"What about these?" Austin held up two sticks decorated with silver ribbons and red and blue stars. "They kind of look like sparklers."

"What do you say we put those on the corners of the front bumpers?"

He eyeballed the location. "How?"

"I'll figure it out in a minute, honey. You keep working on that bunting. We haven't got much time."

He carefully attached each width of red, white and blue plastic, his face downcast. "Where do you think Dad is?"

She wished she knew. "Do you want to try knocking on his door? Maybe he overslept."

"But his truck's gone."

"Well, maybe he went somewhere last night and had to park farther away."

"Okay. I'll check." Head hung low, her boy scuffed across the gravel. It didn't take a genius to figure out he was one disappointed kid. Austin had been looking forward to spending this day with Trent for weeks.

So have you.

"He didn't answer." Austin returned in the same manner he left.

How could Trent let Austin down like this? So not cool.

The last streamer had barely been taped into place when Jenna arrived with her parents. The sun sparkled off of her her rhinestone-encrusted crown and glittery sash. She talked sweetly to Austin, who appeared quite smitten with the seventeen-year-old.

"I spread a blanket over the back-row seat so you won't have to worry about getting dirty." Blakely pointed.

Mr. Hightower, a tall, thin man whose well-worn cowboy boots hinted at rancher, gave the vehicle a visual once-over. "This is cleaner than the car we drove down here."

"I like the pink." Jenna's grin revealed a perfectly straight set of whiter-than-white teeth.

"It matches your sundress." She turned to Jenna's parents. "Mr. and Mrs. Hightower, you're welcome to ride in either the first or second row."

"Where's this young fella gonna ride?" Jenna's father ruffled Austin's hair.

"With my mom." He poked a thumb in Blakely's direction.

"If everybody's ready, it's about time to get on up to the starting point." Again, she scanned the area but saw no sign of Trent.

Jenna's father helped her in first and then his wife.

Blakely slipped behind the wheel as Austin slammed the passenger door. She couldn't help noticing the way he kept watching, waiting for Trent. The guy could have at least called. That is, unless he wasn't able.

She put the truck into Reverse, refusing to give in to the building angst. Trent was okay. Wherever he was.

And, boy, would she be ready to give him a piece of her mind.

Ouray had the best Fourth of July celebrations. And Trent had already missed two of its high points—the pancake breakfast and the parade.

Was he ever going to have a lot of explaining to do.

He had trouble finding a parking spot. When he finally did, he jogged two blocks to Adventures in Pink. The truck he was supposed to decorate was parked out front, streamers still flying, but Blakely and Austin were nowhere to be found. He dialed her cell but no answer.

He hurried up the alley to the motel. Flags flew prominently and star-spangled pennants adorned the railings. He spotted Rose roaming from one pot of red, white and purple flowers to the next, a watering can in hand.

"Mrs. D." He stopped outside the office, winded. "Are Blakely and Austin here?"

She plucked a couple of dead blooms. "You just missed them. They headed up to the Elks Lodge to grab some lunch."

He glanced at his watch. Was it lunchtime already?

Moving closer, she set the watering can on the deck. "I hear you missed the parade."

"Yeah." He raked a hand through his hair. "They called me to the hospital around four this morning. I kept thinking I'd be back in time, but…"

"Things happen. Not much we can do about them."

"If they get back before I find them, will you have her call me, please?"

"I will." She regarded him, wisps of white hair dancing around her face. "Though I might warn you that my granddaughter is a tad upset."

"A tad? I bet that's like saying the Titanic was a little mishap."

He picked his way toward the south end of Main Street, scanning the crowds, maneuvering around one person after another. American flags snapped in the warm breeze as the sun blazed down from a cloudless sky. This could be the hottest day they'd had all season. Though probably not as hot as Blakely's temper.

The aroma of grilling meat pulled him toward the lodge.

He dodged past a long line of people waiting for barbecued ribs and stopped.

Sitting cross-legged on the grass, Blakely played peekaboo with a stroller-bound baby. She wore an Adventures in Pink

T-shirt over a pair of pink, brown and white plaid shorts. With her hair in braids, she looked like a teenager.

Not far away, Austin munched on a hamburger. The poor kid didn't look very happy. And it killed Trent to know he was the reason why.

He took a deep breath and continued onto the grassy area.

"Dad!" Austin leaped to his feet and rushed him, hugging Trent's waist with his free arm. A move that nearly knocked Trent over.

He wrapped an arm around the boy's shoulder. "Sorry I'm so late, buddy."

"Where were you?"

Blakely watched him, her fiery gaze narrowing as she stood to join them.

"I was at the hospital in Montrose."

Austin scrunched his nose. "Are you okay?"

"Of course I am. One of my patients had an emergency. I had to wait on the cardiologist."

"And you couldn't have called? Texted?" The fire in Blakely's blue eyes had diminished to a smolder.

"I had every intention of making it back in time. I really wanted to be a part of everything."

Their gazes shot skyward as a biplane buzzed Main Street, leaving a loop-de-loop contrail in its wake.

"That's okay." Austin smiled. "You didn't miss *everything*."

Trent turned his attention to Blakely, knowing she wouldn't be so quick to forgive. "When I'm at the hospital, I'm in doctor mode. Sometimes I zone out on other stuff."

She crossed her arms over her chest. "Your son is more than 'other stuff.'"

"I get that. But he doesn't seem to be the one with the problem." He stepped closer. "Why are you so upset, Blakely?"

She twisted sideways. "For someone so smart, you sure can be dense."

Moving behind her, he lowered his head until his mouth was right beside her ear. "Then why don't you lay it out for me."

Goose bumps erupted down her arm. "I was worried about you." Her words were barely above a whisper.

"Really?" He couldn't help smiling as he moved in front of her. This was definitely a move in the right direction.

"Yes, really."

"Mind if I borrow this?" He tugged the paper napkin from her hands. "Hold still."

"What?" Her annoyance had yet to fully dissipate.

"Just be still." He wiped a streak of red barbecue sauce from her cheek. "There." He revealed the smudge. "I didn't think you'd appreciate walking around town with that on your face."

The corners of her mouth twitched, that adorable blush coloring her cheeks. "Thank you." She took the napkin and swatted him on the arm with it. "Next time you'd better at least leave a note."

"I promise."

Chapter Eighteen

Blakely and Taryn walked into the roped-off intersection of Main and Sixth Avenue to the sound of cheers. People gathered along all four sides of the crossroads, waiting for the show to start.

Surveying the crowd, she searched for her boy, bypassing the north and south perimeters where the diehards gathered, eager to get soaked by a direct hit from the fire hoses. It took her only a moment to spot Austin, top row of bleachers on the west side, between Trent and Gran.

He sent her a big thumbs-up, a gesture she readily returned.

Gran held a green golf umbrella, her standard accessory for the event.

Trent waved, his biceps bulging, making the Adventures in Pink shirt she'd given him look better than ever.

Panning left, her heart launched into her throat.

Nicole sat on the other side of Trent, her red halter top exposing a little too much skin. She laughed at something Trent said. Tossed her blond ponytail.

Blakely didn't like the twinge of jealousy the sight flared. Then again, Trent's presence had been doing strange things to her insides a lot lately. But he hadn't given her any reason not to trust him.

Taryn had said trust is a choice. Could she choose to trust Trent again?

Shoving aside her jumbled feelings, she readied herself for battle. Like a football player wears pads, she and Taryn put on life vests, the thick cushion a barrier between their body and hundreds of pounds of water pressure. Next, they donned the heavy firefighter garb while Phil Purcell, Taryn's dad and former fire chief, gave them some last-minute instructions.

"Lean into it. Take control right away." He smiled and winked. "They'll never stand a chance."

"We'll do our best, sir." Blakely donned a pink bandanna, tying it at the nape of her neck before pulling on her gloves.

Across the way, their opponents also geared up. Both were younger. Cockier. Kim Barker stood at least five inches taller than Blakely. Her partner, Jackie Reed, somewhere in between. As intimidation tried to set in, Blakely reminded herself that it was technique and skill that would accomplish this—not size.

"You ready, Blakes?" Standing behind her, Taryn lifted the length of fire hose while Blakely gripped closer to the nozzle.

"Ready as I'll ever be."

The hose jerked, growing heavier every nanosecond as it pulsated to life. Blakely struggled to control the movement. This was just a warm-up, so she arched the spray of icy water over the crowd between the bank and Mouse's. Austin would get a kick out of it.

A few seconds later, the hose went limp and they set it on the asphalt while their opponents took their turn.

The current fire chief, Jack Magsig, handed them each a helmet that had been fitted with an eighteen-inch shield to protect their faces from the intense water pressure. Even with the precaution, bloody noses were a common occurrence.

Blakely shoved the helmet on her head and shot up a prayer. As if of its own volition, her gaze drifted to Trent and Nicole. Just because Trent was Austin's father, didn't mean Blakely had any sort of claim. And until recently, she never wanted one. Now...

"Okay, girlfriend. This time it's for bragging rights." Taryn's muffled voice managed to drag her back to reality.

Again, Blakely gripped the nozzle and aimed it in the air as hundreds of pounds of water pressure coursed through the line.

The official's arm dropped.

Game on.

Her aim lowered to their lead opponent's face shield. If she could keep it there, the girl wouldn't be able to see a thing. Wouldn't know where she was aiming.

Water slammed into Blakely's chest. Her shield.

She bobbled and their stream bounced to the opponent's torso.

Against the force of the hose, Blakely struggled to lean forward. Like a good partner, Taryn pressed into her, just like they'd practiced, giving the support she needed.

She hit her target. Held it.

The opposing hose moved left then right. It hit the top of Blakely's helmet, sending icy water down her neck and under her coat.

Still, she kept her mark. Adrenaline moved her forward. Taryn stayed with her.

Now, their opponent's stream seemed to be everywhere but on them.

Shield. Shoulder. Miss.

Gran must be praying hard because Blakely's aim remained steady.

The lead on the other team lost her footing. She tried to switch places with her partner. Bad move. Their hose flailed.

Blakely turned her attention to the second girl's shield.

The girl dipped her head. Now she was staring at the ground while the girl at the rear tried to direct the nozzle. Their stream went up then down. Back and forth. The girl in the second position dropped to her knees. The lead girl fell away completely, sending the hose dancing across the pavement, showering the crowd until officials rushed in to cut the water off.

Blakely let go the breath she hadn't realized she was holding. They'd won. They won?

"We won!" She dropped the nozzle and ditched her helmet at the same second as Taryn. They threw their arms around each other, jumping for joy.

Jack came over and raised their arms into the air, signaling them the winners.

"You did it!" Austin raced toward them and hugged Blakely around the waist.

The crowd continued to cheer as she and Taryn met their opponents at the middle of the intersection for a group hug. Then they shrugged off the heavy gear and padding so the men's teams could take the field. Blakely's clothes were soaked all the way down to her tennis shoes.

On the sidelines, Gran and Trent hollered louder than anybody. Blakely could hardly wait to get to them and share her excitement.

"Your aim was perfect," Taryn all but yelled as they walked out of the spotlight.

"Only by the grace of—"

Thud!

The crowd gave a collective gasp before falling silent.

Blakely shook her head trying to get her bearings. Baskets of red, white and purple flowers dangled from light poles. Asphalt, hot beneath her.

She was on the ground.

Glancing behind her, she realized she'd tripped over the fire hose. How embarrassing. She could hold a hose with five hundred pounds of pressure flowing through it, but she couldn't walk.

She slapped a hand over her face.

"You okay, Blakes?" Taryn looked down at her.

"Yeah. Just get me out of here."

Taryn extended her hand and helped Blakely to her feet. Pain shot up her leg and the next thing she knew she was back on the black top.

Groaning, she reached for her right ankle, trying not to writhe.

Jack dropped beside her, followed by two more firefighters.

"Blakely." Trent pushed into the group, worry etching deep grooves in his brow. "What happened?"

"My ankle." She winced as his skilled hands moved over the already swollen area.

"Somebody get me a cold pack." He straightened her leg, then removed her shoe. "Can you wiggle your toes?"

She did but not without a great deal of pain.

A hand reached through the group, holding what she surmised was an ice pack.

Trent squeezed it a couple of times, breaking the chemical packets inside before laying it atop her foot. "We better get an X-ray."

"There's an ambulance on standby," said Jack.

"No." She bristled. "No, ambulance." She looked into Trent's troubled eyes. "Will you take me?"

He nodded. "I can treat you at the clinic."

She raised her arms slightly, assuming they'd all help her to her feet. Instead, Trent scooped her into his arms and carried her away like some hero in an action movie. Whoops and catcalls littered the air.

She buried her face against his neck. "Trent?"

"What is it?"

"Just shoot me."

An X-ray had confirmed Trent's suspicions. Nothing was broken, but a nasty sprain meant Blakely would be laid up for at least two days. Something she wasn't the least bit happy about.

"I don't see why he even brought the stupid crutches if he's not going to let me use them." Her childish behavior made him chuckle.

"Stop whining." Rose lifted a bouncing Jethro and set him on Blakely's belly. "He'll let you have them as soon as he feels you're ready."

"This is one of my busiest weeks of the season. What am I going to do?" The sheen in Blakely's blue eyes revealed more than her words.

"Now, dear—" Rose laid a hand on Blakely's shoulder. "I'm sure Dan and Lisa will be more than happy to help out."

"I can take care of some office work, if you need me to," Trent added.

"I'll help, too, Mom." Austin spread an afghan over his mother's legs and perched beside her.

"For now, you simply need to be still." The old woman tightened her grip.

"If you prefer, we can tie her down." Trent stood behind the sofa, glancing at Rose.

Blakely glared at him. "I'd like to see you try."

Her grandmother chuckled and strolled toward the motel's office. "I think I'll let you deal with her, Trent."

"My pleasure." He rounded the sofa, realizing how true his words were. He was falling in love with Blakely all over again.

"Here, Mom. You can have the remote." What a kid. He'd make a great big brother. Maybe to a little sister with strawberry-blond hair and melt-your-heart blue eyes.

"Thank you, honey."

"Austin, would you mind checking the coals for me?" Blakely's injury meant a change in plans, so Trent seized the opportunity to grill up some rib eye steaks he'd been saving to treat the Daniels.

"Okay. Come on, Ellie Mae." He patted his thighs. "Come on, girl."

As the door swung closed, Trent knelt next to Blakely. "How you feeling?"

Jethro reached over and licked him.

"Not too bad." She tucked the dog between herself and the back of the sofa. "I just hate being at everyone's mercy."

His gaze held hers as he brushed the back of his finger across her cheek. Sparks flashed between them. "You're used to taking care of everybody else."

Her gentle blush, followed by a hard swallow, told him she felt the connection, too. "That's what I do." The words were barely above a whisper.

"Well, I happen to like taking care of *you*." He leaned closer.

"They're ready." The screen door burst open, and Austin stepped inside.

Disappointment sifted through Trent over the missed opportunity. He sent her a parting smile as he stood.

"Then dinner will be ready soon."

"How's the patient?"

Trent held the front door open for Taryn. "Defiant, despite a severely sprained ankle."

"Don't listen to him, Taryn." Blakely leaned back in her chair. He had agreed to let her join them at the dinner table with the provision her leg remained elevated.

"Actually, your timing is perfect." He grinned at the cute brunette. "Now maybe she won't argue with me about going back to the couch." Skirting the table, he stopped behind Blakely's chair. "Finished?"

With a tilt of her head, she looked up at him. "You're going to act like my personal chariot again, aren't you?"

"Yep."

She pushed her plate away, and he lifted her into his arms, savoring her warmth and the sweet aroma that was uniquely her. He could hold her like this forever and die a happy man.

"Gee, Blakes, must be rough to have some good-looking guy toting you around." Taryn joined them in the living room.

Trent ignored the heat creeping up his neck and settled his favorite patient once again. "See. Now stop complaining."

Taryn perched on the loveseat. "What are you going to do about work?"

"Dad and I are gonna help her." Plate in hand, Austin hopped up from the dinner table and started toward the kitchen. The kid was so proud to be able to help his mom. And Trent couldn't be more proud of him.

"Dan and Lisa and each of her drivers have offered to keep things running for a couple days." Trent cleared his, Blakely's and Rose's dishes.

"Of course they did," said Taryn. "That's what friends do. You know that, Blakes."

"Yeah, I know."

Over the back of the couch, Trent watched Blakely toy with the fringe on the green afghan. Saw the uncertainty in her eyes. Despite the offers of help, she was still worried. No one paid attention to detail quite like Blakely or had a knack for perceiving what a guest wanted before the guest even knew.

And Ross Chapman thought he could buy her out? Trent almost laughed.

Taryn cocked her head and studied her friend. "But you're not comfortable being on the receiving end?"

"I think you hit the nail right on, Taryn." Rose settled into her rocker. "Sometimes we simply have to let go and let God."

"And since Blakely has a hard time letting go, God is forcing her hand." Taryn grinned.

Trent tried to contain his laughter. She had Blakely pegged.

"All right. I get the point." Blakely threw her hands up in the air. "Sheesh. You guys act like I'm not even in the room."

"Well, for what it's worth, Blakes, I'm sorry this happened." Pulling the pillow from behind her, Taryn leaned back, keeping the pillow in her lap. "I guess you're out of commission for the rest of the night, huh?"

Austin dropped into the second rocker. "Yeah, no torchlight parade, no fireworks.... Stinks."

"Yeah, stinks." Blakely's pout matched that of their son. "I mean, what's the Fourth of July without fireworks?"

Trent couldn't bear to watch the disappointment on their faces. Turning, he snagged the remaining silverware from the table and went into the kitchen to load the dishwasher. Austin and Blakely had been looking forward to this day. Rinsing the plates, Trent wished he could figure out a way for them to participate in tonight's festivities.

As he turned off the water, an idea sparked in his brain.

And maybe, with Rose's help, he could actually pull it off.

Chapter Nineteen

Trent would do almost anything to make Austin and Blakely happy. He could only hope she was up for a little adventure.

"Where'd you go?" Austin looked up when Trent walked in the door. With Rose's approval, he'd made his getaway through the motel's office. He should have guessed Austin would notice he was missing.

"I had to run a quick errand."

"Oh." Austin again faced the TV. "Miss Taryn left us a DVD of their win today. Wanna watch?"

"Sure." Trent settled in on the loveseat. He'd have to wait for the right moment to set his plan into action.

Opposite him, a smiling Rose peered over the tops of her reading glasses, her knitting needles moving. She'd loved his idea and provided him with everything he needed.

"Whoa!" Austin pointed at the TV. "You really blasted her good, Mom."

"We did look pretty good out there, didn't we?"

Trent glanced at Blakely. "Must seem kind of surreal watching your victory when only a few hours ago you were in the midst of it."

"A little. Yeah."

The telephone rang and Austin paused the TV. "I'll get it." He rushed to the old rolltop desk. "Hello?"

Trent moved between the sofa and coffee table and knelt down. "How's it going?"

"Hi, Zach." Even from across the room, the dismay in Austin's tone was hard to miss.

"Good." Blakely set a finger to her lips as she concentrated on Austin's conversation.

"No. I can't." He paused. "Yeah. See ya." The frown on his face when he flopped onto the chair was one for the record books.

Blakely turned to look at him. "What did Zach want?"

"He invited me to go with them to the torchlight parade and to watch the fireworks."

She craned her neck to see him better. "Why did you tell him no?"

He shrugged. "I wouldn't feel right leaving you."

"Honey, you don't have to miss out on all the fun just because your mom is a klutz."

Austin smiled at her. "I know." He was something special, all right. Not many kids would ditch their friends for their mom.

This was the moment Trent was waiting for. He pushed to his feet. "Austin, you're going to see the fireworks."

Their gazes collectively landed on him.

"We all are," he continued.

Blakely narrowed her gaze. "Just what do you have in mind?"

"That's for me to know and you to find out. Now do you think you'll be warm enough in those?" He gestured to the pink sweatpants and T-shirt her grandmother and Taryn had helped her change into before he took her to the clinic.

Suspicion sparkled in her subtle glare. "Warm enough for what?"

"It's getting kind of chilly outside. You'll probably want a jacket." He snagged her gray hoodie off the rack by the door.

"I don't know if this is such a good idea. I mean, I have an ice pack on my foot."

"Aw, come on, Mom." Austin was on his feet, his mood considerably improved. "Dad's not gonna let anything happen to you."

Trent saw her indecisive expression. Her pursed lips. "If you're not feeling up to it—"

"Oh, all right. Maybe some fireworks will cheer me up." She pushed up on her elbows. "Austin, better grab your hoodie, too."

"That's the spirit." Rose removed her glasses.

"What about you, Mrs. D?"

"Oh, as much as I would love to join you…" The old woman tucked her needles and yarn into the bag beside her chair. "I plan to be in bed long before those fireworks get started."

"Are you sure?" The last thing he'd want is for Rose to feel unwanted or left out.

"Oh, yes." She stood. "You all have fun, though." Her gaze settled on Blakely. "And tomorrow, I'll want to hear all the details of our sneaky doctor's plan."

After helping Blakely get a running shoe on her good foot, Trent lifted her into his arms, afghan and all. She was so light. Amazing how she was able to hold up against those fire hoses.

"Austin, will you get the door for me?" He carefully maneuvered down the steps and through the front gate.

"Look at the alpenglow." Arms around Trent's neck, Blakely peered over his shoulder. "It's beautiful."

He turned so they could both have a better look.

Sure enough, the gray barren rock of the Amphitheater was painted the most beautiful, yet indescribable, color.

"God has such an amazing way of blending red, orange, amber and violet all at the same time." She let go a contented sigh. "I could never duplicate that with my paints."

He glanced down at her. "Have you tried?"

She smiled. "More times than I care to admit."

He situated her in the passenger side of his pickup while Austin piled into the backseat, then claimed his spot behind the steering wheel. The pink bandanna Blakely had worn this afternoon still sat atop the center console.

"You know, this is supposed to be a surprise." He fingered the thin fabric. "I'd hate to give anything away too soon." He handed it to Austin. "You think we should blindfold your mother?"

Her eyes went wide. "Blindfold? Oh, no you don't."

"Come on, Mom. I won't make it tight."

She searched Trent's face, likely hoping for some indication that he was joking.

He quirked a brow. "You don't trust your own son?"

She huffed and leaned back. "You two sneaks are determined to try my patience tonight, aren't you?"

Austin tied the bandanna around her head. "How's that? Can you see?" He waved a hand in front of her face.

"Not a thing."

"Good." The boy dropped back into his seat.

Trent shifted the truck into Reverse. "Operation Fireworks is under way." Gravel crunched under tires as he backed out of the parking lot. Blakely knew her way around this town like the back of her hand. Even blindfolded, she'd be able to determine where they were pretty quick.

That is, unless he mixed things up a bit.

He moved forward. Made a left. Drove a few blocks, then made another.

"I may not be able to see, but I still know you're on Fourth Avenue."

As he suspected. She had her senses trained on every movement, speculating as to where they were going. Well, he was up to the challenge.

Uphill. Downhill. Slow. Slower. And always the sound of

gravel. Aside from Main, Ouray was a series of gravel streets that perpetually moved either up or down hill, so that wouldn't give away much.

He stopped. Turned again. Right. Left. Right.

In the backseat, a grinning Austin sent him a thumbs-up. The kid was loving this.

"That toe-tapping, ragtime piano music tells me we're close to The Outlaw Restaurant." Blakely straightened as though pleased to have something tangible.

Let her keep guessing.

The music faded as he headed away from Main Street into some of the quieter areas of town.

"Mom, we sure are going to be surprised."

"We? Then how come you're not blindfolded?" The smells of a backyard grill wafted through the window.

"Well—" Trent shot Austin a glance as he made another turn "—we only had one bandanna."

"Yeah." Austin was right behind her. "And it was pink. Guys don't do pink."

"That is not true." She held up her index finger. "What's our motto at Adventures in Pink?"

"Real men aren't afraid of pink." He and Austin rolled their eyes.

Blakely squirmed and fidgeted until he finally pulled into the alley alongside Adventures in Pink and turned the engine off. She started to reach for the blindfold.

"Oh, no you don't." He grabbed her hand, running his thumb over her soft skin, and set it back in her lap.

"You guys are enjoying this way too much."

He watched her, unable to stop smiling. "And it's killing you to be at our mercy, isn't it?"

He hopped out of the cab, his excitement growing by the second. Blakely deserved to be treated special. And he liked being the one to do it.

Meeting Austin at the front of the vehicle, Trent handed

him his keys. "I'm going to need you to unlock and hold the doors for me while I carry your mom."

"This is so cool." His boy snatched the keys and rushed for the door.

"Can I take this thing off now?" Blakely turned in Trent's direction when he opened her door.

"Not yet." He lifted her to him, the sweet smell of her shampoo, the way her body melded with his wreaking havoc with his senses.

He really could get used to this.

He whisked Blakely up the stairwell and through his apartment before settling her atop the pillow and blanket-laden pool chaise he'd borrowed from Rose and now sat on his balcony.

Austin looked like he was about to burst when Trent finally gave him the all-clear sign. "Okay, Mom. You can look now."

Blakely peeled off the blindfold. Her mouth dropped open as she took in her surroundings—the fading blue sky overhead, Hayden Mountain in front and The Western Hotel to her right.

"The apartment?"

He nodded, her approval washing over him. "Outfitted to suit your needs." He stepped out of the way and gestured in the direction of Hayden. "If memory serves me correctly, we'll be front row center for the best show in town this July Fourth."

"You like it, Mom?"

She inspected her makeshift bed. "Like it?" Her gaze found Trent. "I can't believe you went to all this effort—for me. It's perfect."

His heart swelled. Exactly the reaction he was hoping for. Maybe more.

"Hey, look." Austin pointed toward the street and waved. "There's Zach and his family."

The red Jeep stopped in front of Adventures in Pink, and Zach's dad got out.

"Are you sure you don't want to ride in the torchlight parade with us, Austin?" Mark Taylor stared up at them. "We've got an extra seat."

"Austin—" Blakely pushed up on her elbows "—go with Zach. You know you want to."

His frown said he was still struggling.

"We can still watch the fireworks together." She caressed his arm. "Just have them drop you back by here when you're done."

He peered at his mother. "You really don't mind?"

"Not at all."

The smile that erupted on his face was brighter than any fireworks.

"He'll be right down," Trent hollered over the rail.

Austin hugged each of them. "I'll be back as soon as it's over."

"Don't you worry, short man," Blakely yelled after him. "We'll be here."

The door to the stairwell slammed and, a minute later, Austin hopped into the backseat with Zach and waved.

"I think you made his day."

Blakely's long slender fingers took hold of his. Smiling up at him, her blue eyes sparkled like never before.

"I think you made mine."

Blakely stared at Gran's living room ceiling. As soon as her foot was well, she was going to paint that thing. White was too boring and predictable.

Lowering her gaze, she refreshed the screen on the laptop cradled across her middle. No new emails. She groaned. Only ten-thirty and she'd already updated the Adventures in Pink website and responded to all of the emails in her inbox. At this rate, she'd be stir-crazy by noon.

Yesterday wasn't so bad with everyone to keep her company. Now, Gran was cleaning motel rooms and doing laundry, Austin was washing Jeeps at the shop, Trent was working at the clinic and she felt…downright lonely.

Thoughts of Trent brought a smile to her face. The way he'd rushed to her rescue, so caring and attentive. True, he was a doctor and that's what they were supposed to do, but his need to take care of her seemed to transcend his Hippocratic Oath.

And then last night… A satisfied sigh escaped her lips. All that effort so they could watch the fireworks as a family. For all the grief she gave him while she was blindfolded, her heart practically melted when she opened her eyes on that balcony.

Gran was right. In the time Trent had been back, he'd done everything he could to try to make up for the past. But could she really be in love? In only six weeks?

Those questions, as opposed to a sore ankle and lumpy couch, kept her awake most of the night.

God, I'm so confused. My head tells me one thing, but my heart tells me another.

Knock, knock.

Jethro hopped to his feet beside her and did his usual barking bit, while Ellie Mae moseyed toward the door.

"Easy in there. It's just me."

Blakely grabbed hold of Jethro's collar. "Come on in, Lisa."

Her receptionist stepped inside, clutching a stack of papers. "Are you climbing the walls yet?"

"No. Wall climbing isn't on the schedule until this afternoon."

They both got a chuckle out of that.

Lisa perched on the edge of the chenille loveseat. "I assume you're following doctor's orders."

Ellie Mae sashayed alongside her, looking for a rub. Lisa didn't disappoint.

"Oh, yes. Of course, he threatened to duct tape me to the couch if I don't comply."

Dan's wife lifted a hand to cover her laugh. "Sounds like he knows you pretty well."

Embarrassment heated Blakely's cheeks. She cleared her throat. "Whatcha got for me?"

Lisa held out a file folder. "Paperwork."

The blower on Blakely's laptop kicked on, sending a wave of warm air swirling around her as Lisa handed over the papers.

Blakely scanned the routine forms from the forest service. "Could you pass me that pen, please?" She pointed to the coffee table.

Blakely scratched her signature at the bottom. Handed them back. "That it?"

There was another knock on the door, and the canine chorus started up again.

Jethro got away this time. Hopped to the floor.

"Anybody hungry in there?"

Trent?

He was supposed to be at work.

She hadn't even had a chance to freshen up. Bored, she'd unwound her braids but had only finger-combed them since. She needed a shampoo, not to mention a shower.

Running her fingers through her hair, her wide gaze slammed into Lisa's.

Always the encourager, Lisa stood and smiled. "You look fine. And even if you didn't, he'd still be crazy about you." She crossed to the door and opened it.

Trent entered, holding a white paper bag in one hand. "Lisa?"

"Don't mind me. I'm on my way out." She turned and motioned the papers clutched in her hand. "I'll get these in the mail today." She started out the door, then stopped and turned back. "Oh, I almost forgot. A lady from the state called and wants to talk with you. Hope you don't mind, but I gave her your cell number. She said she'd call this afternoon."

"The state, huh? I wonder what that's about." She shrugged. "Guess I'll find out. Thanks, Lisa."

"Later, Lisa." Trent greeted Ellie Mae with a rub.

Not one to be left out, Jethro hopped back on the couch, getting as close to Trent as he possibly could.

"What's in the bag?"

"Lunch." A slate-blue polo shirt added a spark to his dark eyes. Standing at the end of the sofa, he stared at her with a look that practically took her breath away. "How are you today?"

"Bored. Lonely. But other than that, I'm doing great." Yuck. She hadn't even brushed her teeth.

"I figured as much. Only one of the reasons I took the rest of the afternoon off." His smile made her weak in the knees. Which said a lot, since she was lying down.

She grabbed hold of Jethro. "They let you do that?"

"Slow day." He set the bag on the coffee table and placed her laptop beside it. Next, he carefully lifted her bad foot, removed the pillows and sat down, resting her leg on his lap. "I figured maybe God wanted me to hang out with my favorite patient."

Her cheeks grew hot. "What were the other reasons?"

Setting the now-lukewarm ice pack aside, he unwound the elastic bandage, his touch as gentle as it was electrifying. "So I could see for myself how your ankle is doing."

"And?"

He examined it first, poked at it lightly. "The swelling is subsiding. I'd still like you to use the ice, though. At least for today." He grabbed the bandage and started rewrapping.

"When can I stand on it?"

"That remains to be seen." He pulled the afghan back over her feet and draped his arm over her leg. Something that felt completely normal and comfortable.

"How come you're being so nice to me? I mean, I didn't exactly give you a rousing welcome when you first arrived in Ouray."

"I wouldn't have expected you to. But I happen to think you're an amazing woman with a big heart." He rubbed her calf, triggering sensations best ignored. "You deserve to be treated special."

The warmth in his gaze told her there was no reason to question his sincerity.

"However, you never answered my question."

"Question?"

"Are you hungry?"

She grinned. "Starving."

When they'd finished eating, Trent took their trash to the kitchen. Blakely was struggling to find a more comfortable position when she caught him looking at a picture of Austin on the wall between the dining and living room.

"That's one of my all-time favorite photos of him," she said.

"Looks like he's at the beach."

"Yep. Florida. He was two. He's chasing seagulls."

He studied the image awhile longer. "I missed so much." Longing filled his voice. He'd never be able to recapture the years he lost.

Her mind wandered to all the photos she'd taken over the years. Perhaps she could help fill in the blanks.

She pointed to the shelf in the corner. "See all those scrapbooks over there? Why don't you grab the light blue one on the left and bring it here."

When he returned, she set Jethro on the floor and made room for Trent to sit beside her. He rested the book on his lap but didn't open it. Then she saw he was waiting for her.

"Go ahead." She nodded to the book.

He lifted the cover, revealing a photo of her holding a newborn Austin and one of the baby alone. "Look at all that hair." He caressed the picture almost reverently.

"He was born with a full head of dark hair. Used to drive me crazy because it stuck straight up. Even now his curls can get unruly sometimes."

"Tell me about it." He ran a hand over his own hair.

Reaching up, she fingered his dark curls. "Yep, Austin's are soft but thick, just like yours."

He pointed to the picture with her. "You look tired."

"Well, yeah. Twenty-two hours of labor will do that to you."

"Twenty-two? You must have been worn out." Compassion and regret filled his gaze.

She turned the page.

When they'd finished that album, they moved on to the next. Over the next few hours she shared snapshots of her life with Austin that no one outside of her family had ever seen. She'd opened the deepest part of her and allowed Trent access. Raising the question she'd long wanted to ask him.

"Did you love her?"

He stared at her as though not sure how to respond.

She touched his hand. "The truth."

"Not at first. But over time, I chose to love her." He clasped her fingers in his. "When I started going to church, I knew that was what I had to do. She was my wife."

Blakely didn't want to feel the ache that throbbed in her chest. But what had she expected him to say? That he'd lived with this woman for years and never cared about her? Would she have wanted him if he had?

She tugged at the fringe on the afghan draped over her legs. "So what happened?"

"She said I was boring." He moved the last book to the coffee table. "That I cared more about God and my studies than I did about her."

"Was that true?" She shifted to see him better.

"I honestly don't know, Blakely. I thought I was doing the right thing. Trying to be the best husband and provider I could."

"Did you ignore her?"

"I don't think so. At least, not on purpose." He dropped his head against the back of the sofa. Stared at nothing. "But I wasn't giving her the kind of life she wanted or expected when she married me. She was a party girl and expected me to be a party guy." His grip tightened. "When I didn't conform… well, eventually she decided to find someone who would."

She stroked his arm. "I'm sorry. I know that must have hurt."

He looked down at her. "I've had a lot of time to get over it. And finding you and Austin is proof of God's goodness and mercy."

Her smile was a nervous one. Despite all her efforts, Trent had breached her heart once again. She *was* in love.

Laying a hand to his cheek, she tugged him toward her until their lips met. Last night's fireworks paled in comparison. His kiss left her as breathless as a hike to the top of Mt. Sneffels.

She pulled away, leaning her forehead against his. "Gran says we serve a God of second chances."

He kissed her nose. "Your grandmother is a very wise woman."

"I'm ready to give us a second chance."

"Blakely, I have something to—"

Her phone rang.

She pulled back. "Sorry. I need to get that."

He grabbed her cell from the coffee table and handed it to her.

"Hello."

"May I speak with Blakely Daniels?"

"This is she." Her gaze drifted across the room, out the window.

"My name is Greta Malone. I'm with the Colorado Department of Revenue."

"I see." She was pretty sure her heart stopped beating. *Don't panic. Don't…* She grabbed hold of Trent's hand.

"I'm calling to let you know that Adventures in Pink has been selected for an audit that will begin on July twentieth."

Blakely's mouth fell open. Disbelief churned in her gut. "July twentieth? That's impossible. That's our busiest week of the year. There's no way I can possibly—"

"I'm sorry, Ms. Daniels, but unless our schedule changes, July twentieth it is."

Ending the call, Blakely didn't know whether to cry or scream. Looking at Trent, she knew both were inevitable.

"I'm being audited."

Chapter Twenty

Overlooking Twin Peaks from the second floor of The Alps, Trent nursed his third cup of coffee. For someone who pulled thirty-six-hour shifts in the E.R. for three years, he'd sure gone soft fast. What had he been thinking, telling Austin he and Zach could have a sleepover at his place? On a Friday? After a long day at the clinic?

Now he knew why they called it a sleepover. Any hope for sleep was over.

Somebody should have warned him.

Okay, perhaps Blakely had. But he wanted to give her the night off. Wanted her nice and rested when she took the doctors and their families out on that all-day tour. A tour Scott and Rebecca would be on. Which is why he stayed in his apartment until after the tour left. If they'd seen him, the conversation would have been all about the new practice. But since he still hadn't said anything to Blakely...

Their relationship seemed to have turned a corner in the two weeks since her fall. His feelings were growing stronger than he'd ever imagined. But he had yet to tell her he'd be leaving. He couldn't seem to get the words out. Like saying it would make it more real. Inevitable.

Good thing Scott was staying in Telluride.

The laughter of two little boys drew his attention to the sidewalk below. Austin raced behind Ellie Mae while Zach urged Jethro to keep up. They disappeared into the house, only to emerge moments later without the dogs. They continued past the pool, chattering all the way.

"Hey, Dad," said Austin as the two boys clomped up the wood steps. "Can you take us on a hike up to Chief Ouray Mine?"

"Sorry, bud. No can do. I'm waiting for Dan to help me finish moving furniture." Thanks to someone's poorly trained and unattended dog, Rose had to have the carpet replaced in one of the rooms. The furniture had been stored in the adjacent room, meaning both had to be made ready for guests tonight.

"What about after you're done?"

How could they even think about making such a hike? They'd had less sleep than him.

"Not today." He'd be lucky if he had enough energy to complete the task at hand. "Besides, that's a long hike that needs to be started early." He glanced at his watch. "It's already noon."

Austin pouted.

"Sorry, I'm late." Dan waved across the small parking lot.

"No problem." He chugged the rest of his coffee as Dan trotted up the stairs.

"It won't take that long, Dad. Please?"

"Austin! I said not today." His tone was sharper than he'd intended. Chalk it up to lack of sleep.

Dan peered into the empty room. "So that all we got?"

"I already moved the light stuff, but the dresser and beds are a two-man job. Once we get those into the other room we'll need to readjust things in here." Everything had been pushed against the walls to make space for the extra items.

"Let's get to it, then." Dan went into the crowded room while Trent set his cup on the railing.

Austin and Zach were still there. Their faces as long as he'd ever seen them.

He pulled a pair of leather work gloves from his back pocket, remorse kicking him in the gut. "Look, I'm sorry I snapped."

"Can me and Zach go hiking?"

They were bored. And he had work to do.

"Where?"

Austin shrugged. "I dunno. Maybe Cascade Falls or the perimeter trail."

His gaze skimmed Oak Street and Box Cañon. He'd forgotten about the perimeter trail that circled town. Easy, yet time-consuming.

He let go a sigh. "Yeah. Go ahead. Just be back by five."

Trent grunted under the weight of the dresser as he and Dan eased it through the door of the vacant room. Even though they'd removed the drawers, the solid-wood piece weighed a ton.

"Beneath the mirror?" Dan asked.

"Yeah."

They settled the low chest in its place, then returned to the next room.

"Sounds like things are going pretty well with you and Blakely." Dan grabbed two drawers.

Trent did, too. "You'll get no complaints from me." He followed Dan out one door and into the next.

"You're good for her, you know?" His friend slid in his pair of drawers.

"Funny, I would have thought it the other way around." Trent took his turn and started back the way they came.

"Perhaps. But you're not afraid to step in and take control. She needs that sometimes."

Trent grabbed the flat-screen TV. "She does have a tendency to think she's some kind of superwoman."

Dan took the lamp and folding luggage rack. "Oh, you noticed?"

Trent grinned over his shoulder as he exited the first room.

"So are you looking at the future?"

Moving across the cushy green carpet that Blakely had informed him was sage, he felt his stomach muscles tighten. "There's something I should tell you, Dan." He set the television into place and plugged it in. "Something I've failed to tell everyone. Including Austin and Blakely."

Dan plugged in the large lamp on the opposite end of the dresser. "Sounds serious."

Jamming his hands in his pockets, he looked at his friend. "I'm only in Ouray for the summer. I head back to Albuquerque September first." He told Dan about his promise to Scott and the plans they'd made. "When this all started, I didn't even know Austin existed. But I love my son. I want a relationship with him."

"I'm sure you and Blakely can work something out." Dan leaned against the doorjamb.

"But at what cost?" His gaze drifted beyond the window to two hummingbirds zipping around a feeder. "You see, Dan, I love Blakely, too."

Dan blew out a breath. "Sounds like you're torn between two dreams."

"Yep. I got everything I ever wanted. Too bad they're in two different states."

The drive over Black Bear Pass had been as exhausting as it was invigorating. Blakely was glad she'd worn her hiking boots, giving her ankle a little extra support. With her nonstop use of the clutch, brake and gas pedal, she could have been in much worse shape.

By no means was she complaining, though. The group Trent had sent was so large she needed all seven of her tour trucks to accommodate them. Now, guests from the other six tours waited in front of the little blue building on Seventh Avenue as the remainig nine climbed out the back of her truck. Fortunately, their shuttle to Telluride had yet to arrive.

She stepped onto the curb. "Did everyone have fun?"

The resounding "yes" was music to her ears.

"Do I still get a stickuh, Miss Blakely?" The darling four-year-old girl who had been on her tour stared up at her.

How could anyone resist this adorable child? "Of course you do, sweetheart. It's inside." She glanced at the child's parents. "Do you mind?"

"Are you kidding? She's been looking forward to this since this morning," said her father.

Blakely held out her hand and the little blondie took hold. Oh, how she missed this age. Not until recently had she allowed herself to dwell on the prospect of having more children. With Trent in the picture, though, and knowing his desire to have more kids, the thought crossed her mind a lot.

The little girl, who was dressed in pink but had a definite tomboy streak, accompanied her up the concrete steps and inside the building, followed closely by her parents.

"Hey, Lisa." Blakely dropped her clipboard and empty water bottle on the counter. "This is my friend, Daisy." She reached across the desk for a small basket of stickers.

"Well, hi there, Daisy. Did you have fun in the mountains?"

The child nodded emphatically as Blakely stooped to her level and fingered through the options. "Would you like a princess one? Tinkerbell?"

"What's this?" The little girl pulled out a sticker.

"That's a Jeep like that one out there." She pointed out in front of the building to one of her rentals.

"I like it." Daisy grinned, scrunching her nose in the cutest manner.

"Oh, a girl after my own heart. In that case, you can take two."

"Look—" She held them up to her parents. "I got two *Jeeps*."

"You sure do." Her father lifted her into his arms.

"I'm so glad Trent told us about this. Makes me wish we

were staying in Ouray instead of Telluride." Daisy's mother smiled. "I can see why he was so eager to spend a few months here."

"A few months?"

"Yes, he and Scott—" she pointed to her husband "—are opening a new practice in September."

"Shuttle's here." Her husband started toward the door with Daisy.

"New—" Confused, Blakely followed them. "Where is this new practice?"

"In Albuquerque." He paused just outside the door. "Trent and I have been looking forward to this since medical school. Finally, our dreams are coming true."

Blakely's heart skidded to a stop.

"I'll be in my office," she announced when the family departed. She would not cry. Would *not* cry.

Lisa fell in line behind her. "Maybe it's not what you think."

Blakely whirled. "What I *think* is that I've been duped. Again."

The door to the garage flew open just then. She turned as Trent pounded up the steps.

"How dare you." She shoved both hands against his chest. "You were playing me all along, weren't you? Why didn't you tell me you were going back to Albuquerque?"

"I can't find Austin."

"Don't try to—" She paused as his words registered. "What do you mean you can't find him? He probably went on home. Or to Zach's."

"I already checked." The rapid rise and fall of his chest said he'd been running.

"You…went to Zach's?"

"Right after I checked with your grandmother."

Panic swelled inside her, twisting her insides. "When was the last time you saw him?"

"Around noon. I told the boys they could go on a hike—"

She held up a hand. "Wait a minute. You told them they could go on a hike? Alone?"

"Just the perimeter trail. And I gave them instructions to be home by five."

"That was more than half an hour ago." Fear, anger and betrayal collided into one pulsating emotion. "Austin is never late." She pushed past him, stormed through the storefront, pausing at the desk for a set of keys, and hobbled out the door. Once outside, she whirled to face Trent. "Why didn't you go with them?"

"I was helping your grandmother put those rooms back together. The boys were bored."

"That couldn't have taken you more than a couple of hours. They could have waited until you were done."

"Blakely…" He put his hands on her shoulders. A move that would have calmed her yesterday.

"Don't Blakely me." She shoved out of his grasp. Ignoring the pained look on his face, she jerked open the door to the Jeep.

"I'm sorry." He raked a hand through his hair. "How'd you find out?"

"That doesn't matter. What matters is that my son is missing." She paused, her hand on the open window. "And to think I trusted you."

She climbed inside and slammed the door.

"Where are you going?"

"To look for Austin." She pushed the clutch, twisted the key in the ignition.

"Let me go with you."

"No." She glared at him. "You stay away from me. And stay away from my son."

Chapter Twenty-One

Trent watched Blakely's pink Jeep disappear in a cloud of dust. It seemed no matter how hard he tried to get things right, he always messed up.

Blakely's words only aggravated the gaping wound his actions had inflicted. Maybe he wasn't cut out to be a father.

But he would find his son.

Gravel crunched behind him.

"Trent?" Mark Taylor, Zach's dad, ground his red Jeep to a stop. "Any luck?"

He approached the vehicle, shaking his head. He struggled to look the guy in the eye.

Mark nodded toward the passenger seat. "Hop in. We'll take a look around."

Trent complied, though he suspected Mark might want to drive him off a cliff for being so careless with his son.

"This isn't so unlike our boys, you know." Mark shifted gears. "They probably lost track of time. Don't beat yourself up."

According to Blakely, though, Austin was never late. "I shouldn't have let them wander off alone."

"It's not like they haven't done it before."

He sent Mark a curious look. "They've hiked alone before?"

"Around town. Sure."

"Still, they should've been back by now."

"Lots of adventure around Cascade Falls." Mark turned up Eighth Avenue. "Maybe they got distracted up there."

They parked and exited the Jeep, scanning every tree, rock and person for any sign of their sons.

Picking their way up the path, they passed a family of four.

"Excuse me." Trent stopped them. "By any chance have you seen two young boys? One's dark haired with curls, the other sandy haired with a buzz cut."

Four sets of eyes silently conferred before shaking their heads.

"Sorry," offered the dad.

Trent knew it had been a long shot, but that didn't stop the wave of disappointment that rolled over him.

He and Zach's dad continued over the small wooden bridge that led to the other side of the stream.

"Let's check up top." Mark moved left, around a series of boulders. "I know Zach likes the view. Not to mention the spray of the falls."

As warm as today had been, he could see that appealing to two young boys.

But their efforts proved fruitless. The rocky outcropping was empty.

Moving to the edge, they surveyed the area below. A handful of people moved in and around the falls, none of them Austin or Zach.

Returning the way they came, Mark paused at a trailhead. "If they did hike the perimeter trail, they'd have come through here. Mind if we take a look?"

"It's worth a shot."

They wandered into the dense forest of cedar and pine, eyes glued to the dusty trail. With dusk settling in, they were left with only shadowy light.

"Some of these tracks look small enough to be theirs." Mark

knelt, using the tiny flashlight on his keychain for a better view. "But I can't be certain." He stood, the beam highlighting something at the edge of the path.

"What's that?" Trent moved forward and stooped to pick up the object.

His knife.

Hope ignited. His gaze darted around the area as he held out his hand to show Mark. "I gave this to Austin for his birthday."

"That means they were here." Mark cupped his hands around his mouth. "Zach? Austin?"

Trent glanced behind him, then up ahead. "Where does this trail lead?"

"Lots of places. The campground, Portland Trail, Upper Cascade—"

"Chief Ouray Mine?"

Mark's gaze narrowed. "Yes, why?"

"The boys asked me to take them there."

Blakely drove up and down the streets of Ouray. North to south, east to west. Past motels, shops and restaurants. The parks, the school, the hot springs. As she drove, she prayed and called everyone she could think of to ask if they'd seen Austin or Zach.

Her heart wrenched. Where could they be?

Making another slow pass of Main Street, she searched the weekend crowds. Austin was the sun of Blakely's solar system. Losing her mom and dad had been tough. If she lost Austin…

And what about Trent? She'd lost him, too.

No, she never had him.

Blinking back tears, she pulled up to the motel. *God, show me what to do.*

Zach's mother rushed out Gran's front door, stopping when she saw the empty backseat. Blakely recognized her own angst on Shawna Taylor's face.

She stepped out of the Jeep and slammed the door. "I guess they haven't shown up back here?"

On the stoop, her grandmother hugged herself and shook her head.

A red Jeep whipped alongside Blakely's and Trent bolted from the passenger side.

"I think I know where they went." Worry lined his brow, and the distress in his voice told her he was every bit as concerned about Austin as she was.

Of course, he was. It was her he didn't want.

"Where?"

"Chief Ouray." He pointed toward the old mine on the town's northeastern slope.

"Austin wouldn't attempt a climb like that without an adult." The vise on her heart tightened. Or would he? "What makes you think they'd go there?"

"Because that's where they wanted me to take them. Only after I said no did they ask about hiking alone." He reached into his pocket and held out his hand to reveal the knife he'd given Austin.

"He's carried that everywhere since the day you gave it to him. Where did you find it?"

He explained that he and Mark had searched near the falls. "Do you think they'd attempt that by themselves?" His gaze flicked between her, Mark and Shawna.

"You know how fascinated Austin is with mines." Blakely rubbed her arms, suddenly chilled. Daylight faded by the minute, adding to her desperation. She traced the Amphitheater. Bears and mountain lions roamed these mountains.

"Zach, too." Shawna clutched her husband's biceps.

Gravel spewed as another doorless Jeep ground to a stop.

Taryn vaulted out. "I just heard." She hugged Blakely. "Any sign of them?"

She filled her friend in on Trent's suspicions.

"Sounds like a fair assessment. We still ought to cover the Perimeter Trail, though."

"Shawna and I can do that," said Mark. "Start at the same point, go opposite directions and meet in the middle."

"Smart idea," said Taryn. "I'll come, too."

"Blakely and I can head toward the mine." Trent toed some gravel that had made its way onto the sidewalk, then cut her a quick glance. "If that's all right with you."

What could she say? She had to find her son. Even if it meant being with the man who betrayed her.

She nodded.

"What about your ankle?" He thrust his hands in his pockets. "Think you can make it?"

"I don't care if I have to crawl. There's no way I'm staying behind."

"Mom! Dad!"

Their gazes collectively jerked toward Main Street.

Zach raced down the sidewalk, tears streaking his dirty cheeks.

Blakely's hopes soared. Her boy was safe.

But where was he?

Panic gripped her once again as Mark and Shawna scrambled to meet their son. Hugged him.

"Where's Austin?"

Chapter Twenty-Two

Zach pulled free, his breathing fast and jerky. "In the mine. He needs help."

In the mine? Trent didn't want to think about the ramifications. He just knew that he had to get to his son.

Within minutes he'd shifted into action along with the others. Darkness shrouded Ouray as they filled their packs with water bottles, flashlights and whatever else they could grab on a moment's notice.

While Taryn pulled together a rescue team, Trent followed the Taylors and Blakely up the side of the mountain. After an hour of climbing, every tree and switchback mirrored the one before. The grueling pace made his leg muscles feel like they were on fire. But frustration and regret propelled every step.

Despite the cool air, sweat spilled down the side of his face. He wiped it with his sleeve. The moon had yet to rise above the Amphitheater and, save for the LED beams of their headlamps, blackness pressed in on every side.

Images of his son, scared and alone, plagued him. What had possessed him to let those boys go off by themselves?

The night breeze rustled through the pines, and cricket chirps filled each excruciating moment. A layer of powdery earth and gravel gave beneath their feet, sending small billows of dust into the air.

Blakely trudged ahead of him. She'd given in to a slight limp on the last switchback, but he knew better than to bring attention to it. Besides, she hadn't said a word to him since they left the house. He'd failed her once again, this time risking the life of their son.

Would she ever forgive him?

"You…okay back there?" Blakely's voice yanked his mind to the here and now. Her breathing was ragged. Then again, they were moving at a good clip. Not to mention they'd probably climbed a thousand feet in elevation.

"I could ask you the same thing." His words rushed out in a single breath.

An owl hooted in a nearby tree.

Blakely startled, stumbled backward, catching her bad foot on a tree root.

Trent caught her, but pain was evident in her pinched expression.

"Everything all right?" Mark, Shawna and Zach stopped and looked back.

"Keep going." Trent settled Blakely to the ground. "We'll catch up." Kneeling, he untied the laces of her hiking boot.

"I'm okay. Really." The way she winced when he removed her boot didn't do much to prove her claim. Her foot had barely healed as it was. At this point, any trauma was a setback.

"No you're not." He dropped his backpack and retrieved an elastic bandage. "I grabbed this, just in case." He eased off her sock, trying not to think about the softness of her skin as he wrapped the foot and ankle snug enough to give her some support.

"See how that feels." While she put her shoe back on, he slipped off the path, just far enough to find something that might help her.

She was standing when he returned, testing the foot. "It's stronger."

"Good." He handed her a long stick. "This will help with your balance and maybe allow you to take a little pressure off of that foot."

Her gaze quickly slipped to the ground. "Thank you."

A crescent moon had risen above the Amphitheater by the time they caught up to the Taylors. Its feeble beams morphed the blackness into an ominous blue-gray. They still had so far to go and all the while Austin was trapped in utter darkness. Scared. Cold. Hungry.

The trail curved westward until they were looking down on Ouray. Lights flickered across the tiny town, reminding him they were not alone. People were praying. Empowering them to press on.

He could do this. He closed his eyes. He *had* to do this.

The slope grew steeper around the next turn. Loose stones shifted and scattered.

The sound of rushing water.

Cascade Creek.

They were almost there.

Blakely practically ran now, albeit with a hitch in her step.

Ahead, white water plummeted past jagged rocks to the stream below. Giant chunks of stone and logs scattered along and throughout the narrow creek, creating more than one easy means of reaching the other side.

A few moments later, they passed the old bunkhouse, a crude structure of corrugated metal and hand-hewn boards.

Another building loomed ahead. Perched on the mountain-side, the windowless metal structure that had once served as machine house for the mine remained a fixture that was visible some two-thousand-plus feet below in Ouray.

"Okay, gang…" Mark sucked in a breath. "This is where things get a little tricky, so pay close attention."

He wasn't exaggerating. The trail descended sharply. Rocky terrain with little to no vegetation.

Trent swallowed the dread that threatened to stop him in his tracks. He didn't recall this part of the hike being so difficult. Traversing it during daylight hours would have been a feat in and of itself. In the dark, however....

Sometimes moving at a snail's pace, he never let Blakely more than one or two steps in advance of him.

Zach rushed ahead. "Over here. Hurry."

Mark followed his son down the short embankment, while Shawna moved aside, allowing Trent and Blakely to pass. Trent hopped down first, then slid his hands around Blakely's waist to ease her beside him.

Tailings, dynamited rock that had been removed from the mine, ground beneath their feet as they inched their way onto the small outcropping.

His foot slipped. Though he managed to catch himself, Blakely latched onto his arm. A move he wasn't about to analyze.

He took a deep breath and continued, trailing his flashlight around a V-shaped cluster of pine trees, down to two large rocks.

His muscles tightened.

Zach lay on his belly to peer inside the rough opening that had been cut into the mountain. "Austin? I'm back. You okay?"

"Looks like an airshaft." Mark fixed his flashlight on the eighteen- to twenty-inch hole.

"For the mine?" Trent dropped onto the dusty earth. Although the opening didn't seem very big, for a small boy like Austin...

"These mountains are riddled with them." Blakely's voice held an air of resignation. "Though they're not usually this big."

Lying prostrate, Trent used his flashlight to peer through the narrow tube, deeper and deeper into the blackness. "Austin?

"Down here." His boy whimpered.

"Do you see him?" Blakely lay down opposite him.

"Not yet." He'd heard about these airshafts, that they could stretch on for hundreds of feet. Bright as his LED flashlight was, it would never shine that far.

To his relief, ten feet down, the rock ceiling gave way to a tunnel. And there, with tearstained cheeks, clutching one arm in the other, was his son.

"Hey there, buddy." His heart lightened as his throat clogged with emotion. "Boy, am I glad to see you."

"I'm sorry, Dad." Austin sobbed. "I know I wasn't supposed to come up here."

The poor kid was worried about being in trouble. "Are you hurt?"

"My arm."

Blakely scooted forward for a better view. "Austin? I'm here, baby." She sniffed. "The Mountain Rescue Team is on their way. You know how you've always admired them. They're going to get you out of here as fast as they can. I love you. You just need to hang on, okay?"

Her words rolled out at warp speed. A nervous mechanism he'd witnessed time and again when he worked the E.R.

"I'm scared," said Austin.

"I know, sweetie." Her voice cracked.

"We're right here, Austin," said Trent. "And we're going to keep shining this light until they get to you."

"He looks cold." Blakely shifted, opened her pack and pulled out Austin's hoodie. She dangled it over the hole.

"Heads up, bud," said Trent. "Here comes a jacket."

She let it drop.

Voices drifted on the breeze. The clatter of carabiners.

He looked up as a series of headlamps bobbed ever closer.

Blakely leaped to her feet. Now she could finally get to her boy. "Over here."

Equipment rattled through the chilly night air.

Taryn rushed toward her. "Is he okay, Blakes?" Despite her years of expertise, Taryn gasped for air. That, coupled with how quickly they'd arrived, told Blakely they'd raced up the mountain.

"I think so." Tears pricked her eyes as she pointed to the hole. "He's…down there." Taryn dropped to her level, motioning to her teammates. "This way, guys."

Clad in helmets and bright orange jackets, the seven volunteers marched passed Blakely. Each had been specially trained in rope rescue, emergency medicine, avalanche and swift water rescue. In the real world, she knew them all. And in all her years of helping them in their fund-raising efforts, she never dreamed she'd be on the receiving end of their services.

Rock ground against rock as they continued toward the only visible sign of her son.

One of the men caught her eye. Shorter than the others, Art Jenkins' thick white hair peeked out the sides of his helmet. The elderly gentleman, with more stamina than people half his age, was one of a handful of retired miners who still lived in Ouray.

"Mr. Jenkins? What are you doing here?"

"I've come to help."

Eric Hoffman stopped alongside the man. "Nobody knows the area up here, or down there—" Eric pointed to the mountain beneath them "—better than this fellow."

Her gaze returned to the old man. "I don't know how to thank you."

"No thanks necessary, young lady."

"We'll need to go in through the mine," said Nolan Dickerson after a quick assessment of the situation. The apparent captain for this venture started back up the rocky slope. "Eric, we'll need those bolt cutters."

Blakely stepped into his path. "I want to go with you."

"Sorry, but I can't allow that." Nolan stared down at her like a father warning a child.

Taryn pushed between them, her pale blue gaze filled with concern. "We'll get him out, Blakes."

"And what am I supposed to do? Sit out here and twiddle my thumbs?"

"Of course not. You pray. Just like everyone in Ouray is doing." Her expression softened. "You're going to have to trust us."

Trust. Something that didn't come naturally. She glanced at Trent.

"Besides—" Taryn rubbed Blakely's arm "—hearing your voice will keep him calm until we get there."

As the team accessed the mine, Blakely snatched the phone from her pocket and dialed Gran. She kept the conversation brief and relayed only the barest of details. She didn't have the energy for any more.

Ending the call, she hurried back to the air shaft. Mark and Shawna clung to their son.

Blakely longed to do the same with her boy. Patience had never been her strong suit. She wanted to touch Austin. Comfort him. Hold him.

"You're hungry, huh?" Trent's voice held a hint of a smile.

"That's a good sign." Looping the strap of her flashlight around her wrist, she again pressed her body against the cold ground and stared into the depths of the mountain.

Trent reached for his backpack, fished inside, then revealed a protein bar. "Incoming," he hollered into the earth before dropping the bar.

"Oatmeal raisin?" Her son's muffled lament encouraged her. "I like peanut butter better. Or chocolate chip."

Trent smiled at her. "I'll make note of that."

Over the next half hour, Trent talked with Austin about everything from sports to movies. She appreciated his efforts to distract their son. Especially since she couldn't seem to do anything but watch Austin, the way she used to when he was a baby. Fearful that something bad would happen and she'd lose him forever. Just like her mom and dad.

Her heart ached. She should have been there. Given Austin her undivided attention instead of gallivanting across the countryside with people she didn't even know.

Maybe Ross was right.

"I hear something." Austin's attention shifted to the tunnel. "I see something."

Blakely held her breath as seconds ticked by.

Finally, her son smiled up at them. "They're here!"

Chapter Twenty-Three

Trent drove Austin and Blakely home from the medical clinic, hoping and praying for a chance to redeem himself.

A sprained wrist and a few bruises were all Austin had to show for his ordeal. Trent couldn't remember when he'd been more frightened. The thought of losing his son at all, let alone right after he'd found him, was more than he could bear. Now every fiber of his being praised God for safely restoring his son to him.

Overall, Austin probably fared better than either Trent or Blakely. All the way down the mountain, he and Zach talked the ears off of the rescue team, not to mention the old miner, Mr. Jenkins. Trauma aside, the kid was ecstatic that he'd been inside an actual mine.

Now, the excitement had finally caught up to Austin. He lay with his head in Blakely's lap, his breathing slow and steady.

Trent watched as she stroked Austin's dark curls. Why hadn't he told her? So many times he set out to, but he'd always let something stop him. There was no such thing as perfect timing. He should've just laid his cards on the table from the beginning. If he had, maybe Blakely would still believe in him.

"When do we tell him?" Blakely's words cut the excruciating silence.

Hands on the steering wheel at ten and two, he focused on the road. In his mind, the question wasn't when but how. He knew Austin would be disappointed. Just like his mother. "Let's give it a day or two. Give him time to move past what happened today."

No response. She simply stared out into the blackness. A car passed from the opposite direction, its lights highlighting the worry lines around her pretty blue eyes. Eyes he'd never again have the opportunity to lose himself in. To stare into their depths, right into the heart of the only woman who would ever truly hold his heart.

"Would it be okay if I carry him up to bed?" He pulled up to the motel and shifted the truck into Park.

She hesitated a moment before nodding.

Trent cradled his son in his arms and went up the walk, into the house and to his room. Austin smelled of earth and little boy, his body relaxed against Trent's.

Emotion pricked the backs of Trent's eyes. Would this be the last time he held his son?

Out in the hall, he caught Blakely at the top of the stairs. "I should have told you. I tried several times, I just…"

She leaned against the wall, arms folded tightly over her chest. "I don't believe you." Her truthfulness sucked the wind out of him. "I think you came here for Austin. But to get to him, you had to go through me."

"You really believe that?" He hoped she'd say no. That she'd remember all they'd shared.

"I think you should go." She headed down the stairs and straight to the door.

He wanted to wrap his arms around her, make her believe in him. In them. But she'd only pull away.

She held the door wide. "Goodbye, Trent."

His heart pounded with regret on the short drive back to his apartment. He had no clue what to do, how to make things right.

Pulling his cell phone out of his shirt pocket he dialed Dan. "Sorry to call so late, but I could really use a friend."

Inside his apartment, he put on a pot of coffee. Had a feeling he was going to need it. About the time it finished brewing, three raps on the door signaled Dan's arrival.

"It's open."

"Smells good." Dan sidled up to the pass-through bar and took a seat.

Trent filled his mug and gestured to the pot. "Care to join me?"

"Why not?" His friend waited as Trent poured. "Rough night, huh?"

"You have no idea."

"Praise God things ended so well."

"That's for sure." Trent would never be able to thank Him enough. He handed off the plain white mug. "Milk or sugar?"

"Both."

He flung open the fridge, grabbed the carton of two percent and set it on the counter. "Wimp." He slid a spoon and a small bag of sugar Dan's way.

"Spoken like a man who takes his coffee seriously." Dan added two spoonfuls and a splash and stirred. "You're lookin' pretty rough."

Trent shrugged. "Nothing a shower and some rest won't cure."

"That'll take care of the outside, but what about the inside?"

He sent his friend a lopsided smile. "That's why you're here." Cup in hand, he headed for the living room. "Austin's disappearance wasn't the only thing that happened today."

Dan twisted around on the barstool. "Oh?"

"Blakely found out I was leaving." He sat on the couch and met his friend's stare. "Only she didn't learn it from me."

Dawning lit in his friend's tired eyes. "I'm guessing that didn't go over well."

"I should have told her, Dan."

"So why didn't you?"

"I don't know. I guess I was afraid she'd react…just like she did." Trent raked a hand through his greasy hair. "And just when I was starting to earn her trust."

"So when's God going to earn yours?"

"What?" He sent Dan an incredulous look.

Leaving his mug on the counter, Dan walked toward him. "Fear held you back from telling Blakely. Fear isn't of God. We're called to step out in faith and trust Him with the outcome."

Cradling the warm mug in his cold fingers, Trent rested his forearms on his thighs and stared at the wood-look floor. "Guess I don't have this trust thing down as well as I thought I did." If he had, he might not be so miserable right now.

Dan settled on the other end of the couch. "God's way may not be easy. But it's always better."

"You're right." Trent took a sip, then set his mug on the side table. "I need to trust Him to work out the logistics of my future with Austin."

Dan watched him. "What about Blakely?"

"Have you not been listening? I blew it. It's over. Kaput."

"So that's it? You're just going to let her go?"

"Well…"

Dan shook his head. "Sorry, Trent, but you're a fool."

"Pardon me?"

"In some ways, you and Blakely are a lot alike. You spend a whole lotta time worrying about everyone else, but what do *you* want? What's important to you?"

He didn't even have to think. "Austin and Blakely. I think God brought me to Ouray for a reason. And more than anything, I'd like for the three of us to be a family."

Dan looked him straight in the eye. "Then what are you willing to do to make it happen?"

Blakely hadn't wanted to come to work Monday morning. She wanted to go back to bed, crawl under the covers and forget that Trent Lockridge existed. How did the old saying go? Fool me once, shame on you. Fool me twice...

Shame on her for listening to her heart and not her head. She knew better. She fought it every step of the way, but in the end Trent still wormed his way back into her heart and her life. Now, here she was, picking up the pieces once again.

"I thought you'd be done crying by now." Taryn strolled through the front door of Adventures in Pink.

Blakely slammed her hand down on the stapler. "I'm not crying." At least not at the moment.

"Then what's causing those red-rimmed eyes?" Her friend rested her forearms on the counter.

"Allergies?" She added the papers to her stack.

"Come on, Blakes. Austin is fine."

She grabbed the next invoice, proof of insurance and credit card receipt. "You're right. Austin is fine." Smacked the stapler again. Set the papers aside.

Taryn scooted around the L-shaped desk. "Don't tell me you're getting all worked up over the audit?"

Blakely had to be one pretty pathetic person when an audit was her only bright spot. "The lady called this morning to say they'd have to postpone it until October."

"How come?"

"Seems they couldn't find a motel in Ouray that fit their per diem."

"In July?" Taryn rolled her eyes. "Gee, imagine that." She leaned her backside against the display case. "Well, at least you got a reprieve."

Blakely nodded and grabbed another tissue. By then Trent would be a distant memory. Or so she hoped.

"What's the problem, then?"

"Trent." She faced the computer. Palmed the mouse. Closed the screen. "He did it again."

"What?"

She took a deep breath, then let it out. "Turns out he's leaving at the end of August." She blinked back the threat of tears, refusing to give in. "He lied to me, Taryn. Led me on, made me fall for him *again,* all without mentioning that he was only here for the summer."

"He *made* you fall for him?"

Turning, she glared at her friend. "You know what I mean." She blew her nose and tossed the tissue in the trash.

"If he didn't tell you, then how did you find out?"

"One of those doctors on Saturday's tour." She inched onto the stool. "Apparently he and Trent are opening a practice together."

Lips pursed, brow puckered, Taryn seemed to contemplate her words. "Maybe Trent was going to tell you. Maybe he was having second thoughts about leaving."

"Or maybe he was trying to butter me up so he could steal Austin out from under me." Blakely slid off the stool.

"You can't really believe that."

Ignoring her friend's remark, she tucked the stack of invoices into a folder, crossed to the files and yanked open the drawer.

"Where is Trent now?"

"Don't know, don't care." He'd come by to see Austin yesterday, but she made certain she was nowhere in sight.

"If that were true, you wouldn't be crying."

Blakely slammed the file drawer closed. "*This* is why I was so guarded. *This* is why I didn't want to give him the benefit of the doubt. But you and Gran, oh, you thought it was divine intervention." She crossed to a display of T-shirts and started folding.

Taryn followed. "Blakes, I agree Trent should have told you he was leaving. But he didn't lie."

"Why are you defending him?"

"Yes, he withheld information, but he didn't lie. His feelings for you are true."

Blakely paused, daring to meet her friend's ice-blue eyes. "And just how do you know that?"

"Because there are some things that can't be faked."

"Like what?" Finished with that display, she moved onto the next.

"Like the adoration in his eyes when he looks at you. The spontaneous smile that erupts when you walk into the room."

She paused her folding. Had Taryn really seen those things?

"The way he's always there whenever you need him."

Blakely confronted her now. "That could have been planned."

"Face it, Blakes. When was the last time a man showed you that much love?"

The door creaked open and Bruce Ball, the driver she lost to Ross Chapman, stepped inside. Like always, he removed his signature brown safari hat and ran a hand through his thick salt-and-pepper hair.

"Hey, Bruce." Taryn waved as Blakely laid the last shirt atop the pile and started toward him.

What was Bruce doing around town on a Monday morning? He should be out on a tour. Unless…

"Taryn." He nodded, then turned his gaze to Blakely. "I heard about the other night. Thought I'd stop in to see how Austin is doing."

"A little banged up, but other than that, he's doing great."

Any other time Bruce would have hugged her. Instead, he clutched his hat in both hands. "That's good to know. The wife and I were praying for him."

"Thank you. We felt every one of them."

An awkward moment passed before the sixty-six-year-old man addressed her again. "I was wondering if I might be able to speak with you."

Taryn jumped and scurried across the blue-gray carpet. "Don't mind me. I was just leaving." She pushed the door open. "Catch ya later, Blakes."

Her former driver strolled around the space like he'd never been there before.

"What's on your mind, Bruce?"

"Things, uh, going okay around here?" He fingered a couple of T-shirts on hangers. "You doin' all right?"

She shrugged. "Can't complain."

He moved on to the display of bumper stickers, his back to her. "Looks like you're keeping plenty busy. I seem to see pink Jeeps everywhere I go."

"Now *that* I like to hear." She wandered to the glass display case and straightened the racks of maps. Something wasn't right here. She'd known this guy all of her adult life and now he could barely talk to her. "How are things up at Mountain View Tours?"

"Not so good." He faced her now, regret marring his weathered features.

"What's the problem?"

"I made a big mistake, Blakely." He seemed to relax as he told her how Ross behaved as though he owned his employees, how he skimped on maintenance. "You know how he offered to double my pay?"

"That's why you took the job." She moved to the snack bar and grabbed two waters from the fridge. "I understand how you couldn't turn that down." Closing the space between them, she held one out to Bruce.

He accepted. "Not only have I not seen an increase, I've seen less. Chapman docks his drivers for anything and everything. If we blow a tire, we pay for it. If we're late coming back from a tour, he docks us for every minute we're late. Now how on earth is a guide supposed to treat his guests to an enjoyable tour when he's worried about losing money?"

Blakely took a sip of her drink. She may not know much, but she knew that was not good business.

"And you know the Active Life Seniors Group out of Grand Junction?"

The one she lost to Ross. "Yes."

"They did not have a pleasant experience at all."

"How come?" She recapped her bottle and set it aside.

"Well, for starters, most of those young fellas over there don't know diddly about the area, so there's no narration. Then the trip was abbreviated because of rain."

"Didn't he have a rain canopy? Ponchos?"

"You know those blue tarps you find at the discount store?"

Her eyes widened. "You're kidding?"

Bruce shook his head. "It definitely wasn't the kind of service the group was used to."

"That's for sure." She moved back behind the desk, appalled that she'd entertained the idea of selling to Ross. No matter how fleeting the thought.

Next year she'd be the one wooing the senior group, and she'd make sure they had the time of their life.

Bruce stepped up to the other side. "One little old lady recognized me from Adventures in Pink and told me I should be ashamed of myself."

"Oh, I'm sorry, Bruce."

"Don't be." His voice was firm, full of conviction. "You and your grandfather have always run a top-notch business. And, to tell you the truth, that woman was right. I should be ashamed of myself. Leaving you like that. You know, sometimes we just don't appreciate what we have until we don't have it anymore."

The comment had her thoughts drifting to Trent. She'd come to rely on him more than she thought. He was her rock. Without him…

"Bruce, have you quit Mountain View Tours?"

"Can't afford to."

She moved to the counter. "But you could if you had another job lined up, right?"

"In a heartbeat."

She smiled. "Adventures in Pink is your home, Bruce. Would you please come home?"

His green eyes glistened with unshed moisture. "I'd be honored to."

The telephone rang.

"Excuse me one sec." She turned on the handset. "Adventures in Pink, this—"

"Mom." Austin was crying.

"What's wrong, honey? Are you okay?"

"Dad's gone."

Chapter Twenty-Four

Monday evening, Trent strode up the driveway of the modest single-story stucco home in northeast Albuquerque, past Scott's ancient Honda Civic. The crossroads of his future lay before him. Only God knew which direction he would take.

With a bolstering breath, he knocked on the door.

A minute later, it swung open and Rebecca smiled out at him. "Trent."

Her four-year-old daughter clutched her leg, all the while eyeing him with a bashful grin.

He sent her a wink, remembering the day she was born. "Hi, Daisy." He'd had the privilege of watching her grow. Something he'd missed with Austin.

The pretty brunette lifted the child into her arms, then stepped aside with a sweeping motion, inviting him in. "We weren't expecting to see you." She leaned in for a one-armed hug. "We'd hoped to meet up with you in Colorado, but they kept us so busy."

"That's all right. Is Scott around?"

"Yeah. Come on in."

Her flip-flops slapped against the tile floor as she led him down a short hallway into the kitchen.

Scott hovered over a pile of papers at the kitchen table.

"Honey, look who's here."

Scott's blond head popped up. "Hey, buddy." Smiling, he pushed to his feet and greeted Trent with a hug and a slap on the back. "I was actually going to call you tonight. Looks like you saved me the trouble."

"Well, I've kind of been looking forward to talking to you, too."

"You won't believe it, Trent." Scott led him into the comfortable living area adjacent to the kitchen. "This thing is taking on a life of its own. Because of our location and our faith-based principles, I've had two established doctors contact me, wanting to know if we're looking for more associates." He plopped onto the red sofa.

"Really? That's incredible." And almost unheard of. Established doctors coming to them? Trent and Scott couldn't have done that if they tried.

Moving aside a baby doll, he joined his friend.

"Yeah. It's crazy."

Trent saw the glint of excitement in his friend's brown eyes. Felt a little excitement of his own. Was this part of God's plan? He prayed so. "How do you feel about bringing on more doctors?"

Scott shrugged. "I think it would give us some great opportunities. More exposure."

"I'm glad to hear you say that." Trent scanned the family photos atop the mantel, thoughts of Austin filling his heart and mind. "Because I learned some things while I was in Ouray."

"Yeah?"

Forearms on his thighs, Trent clasped his hands together. "I have a son, Scott."

"A son? That's…" His friend looked perplexed. "Okay, don't get me wrong, buddy. I'm happy for you. Just a little confused."

Trent spent the better part of the next hour filling Scott and Rebecca in on the treasures he unearthed in Ouray and all that had transpired with Austin and Blakely.

"Oh, Trent. I'm so happy for you." Rebecca sat on the edge of her chair, bouncing Daisy on her knee.

Scott looked serious, something usually reserved for work. "When did you find out about Austin?"

"Less than a week after I arrived in Ouray."

Scott's gaze narrowed. "Then why would you sign off on a practice in Albuquerque? Unless you're bringing him here?"

"No. Austin belongs in Ouray." And so did Trent.

"So why would you...?" His friend's brow puckered with confusion.

"I gave you my word."

Scott's brown eyes went wide. "Seriously? Trent, we're talking about family. I mean, I love you to death, but even you would lose out to my family." He leaned back against the cushions and raked a hand through his short hair. "I can't believe you didn't tell me."

Staring at Scott's family photos, Trent thought back on all the turmoil and indecisiveness. "Me, either."

"So Austin's mom owns the Jeep tour company?" His friend was still trying to piece things together.

"Blakely, yes."

"Strawberry-blonde. Gorgeous. She was great with Daisy."

"She gave me *Jeep* stickuhs," said Daisy.

Trent chuckled. "That's Blakely."

Rebecca smoothed her daughter's blond hair. "Now I understand why she looked so stunned when we mentioned you coming back to Albuquerque."

Scott regarded him again. "Are you in love with her?"

Trent took a deep breath, more certain than he had been in a long time. "Yes. Yes, I am."

"Does she love you?"

A week ago he would have said yes. Now... "I don't know."

Scott glanced to his wife, then back. "Trent, buddy, you gotta find out."

* * *

Pain radiated up Blakely's right leg. She'd done it again. This time tripping over a box in her bedroom.

"Are you okay, Mom?" Austin's eyes were wide as he watched her clutch her ankle.

"I think so." Though she couldn't be certain.

"Wait." Austin held up a hand. "I know what to do. I'll be right back."

She heard him thud down each and every step, say something to Gran, then thud back up each and every one.

"Here." He handed her an ice pack. "You need to keep it on your foot."

"Okay, just a sec." She scooted across the carpet until her back was against the bed. "That's better." She laid the ice pack atop her ankle, then eyed her little man. "Like that?"

"Yep. That's just how Dad did it."

If only Trent were here now. In the week that he'd been gone her emotions had volleyed between regret, anger, disappointment and hope. How she wished she'd taken the time to listen to his side of the story. Then again, he was the one who'd left. Still, he never turned in the key to his apartment. She figured she'd give that one another week. If the first of the month came and went with no rent…

"When did you do this?"

Looking up, she saw Austin standing alongside the box she'd tripped over. The one that usually lived in the back of her closet. He was holding the small canvas she painted of Trent all those years ago.

"That was back when I first knew your dad."

Austin came over and sat beside her, still holding the painting. "I miss him." His head fell against her shoulder. Trent had been good about calling Austin every day, but she knew it wasn't the same.

She leaned her head against his. "You wanna know a secret?" She felt his nod. "I miss him, too."

"Do you think we can ever be a real family?"

As mad as she was that Trent hadn't been completely honest with her, she wanted them to be a real family, too. "I don't know, Austin. I wish I did. We're just going to have to trust that God has a plan."

"Pastor Dan says God's ways aren't like our ways. But that all things work together for good. We just have to trust."

Blakely blinked away the unbidden moisture in her eyes. "He's right." Though trusting was the hard part.

Her boy pushed to his feet. "Well, I'm gonna trust that Dad's coming back. I don't know when, but God knows."

The faith of a child.

She held out her hand. "Want to help me up?" She set the ice pack aside. "I think my foot's better."

When she finally made it to her feet, she knew she was right. Just a little bruise.

"Come on." She snagged the ice pack off of the floor. "Let's go watch a movie."

"I get to pick." Austin was out the door and halfway down the stairs by the time she made it into the hall.

"No superheroes," she called after him. They'd just remind her of Trent. Her heart couldn't take it.

Gran had the popcorn ready by the time the three of them settled on the couch for another viewing of *Ice Age*.

Blakely couldn't get enough of that little prehistoric squirrel.

There was a knock at the door. "I'll get it." Austin popped up, maneuvering around the barking dogs. "Dad!"

Trent? She glanced at her comfy basketball shorts. The ones she only wore when she was sure no one would see her.

The door flew open as Blakely shot to her feet. Her pulse raced. How could Trent have grown more attractive in only a week?

Austin threw his arms around his father.

Trent embraced his son, joy evident in his brilliant smile.

"You have no idea how much I missed you." His gaze lifted to Gran, then Blakely. "All of you."

"It's not dark yet." Austin pulled away. Peered up at his dad. "Maybe we could shoot some hoops."

Trent looked down at him with all the love a father could possess. "Buddy, I am so ready for a game of one-on-one. But right now, I need to talk to your mom."

Her heart leaped somewhere in the vicinity of her throat. "Um… T-to me?"

"Preferably in private."

"Private?" She glanced around the room. Nope. No privacy there.

"Think we could go over to Adventures in Pink? Talk there."

Alone? "Sure. Just let me put on some shoes." And jeans.

The sun had dipped below Twin Peaks, casting shadows over the town as they strode down the alley.

"How have things been going?" Trent shoved his hands in the pockets of his shorts. Relaxed. Casual.

She could only pretend to be calm. "Real good. Remember the driver I lost?"

"You mean the one Ross stole?"

Glancing up at him, she couldn't help thinking how much she'd missed that smile. "Turns out Ross is a lousy boss. So, Bruce is back with me."

"Excellent."

When they reached Seventh Avenue, she started for the front door.

Trent grabbed her hand, the simple touch sending shivers dancing up her arm. "Think maybe we could go to my apartment? The balcony, of course."

"Okay." She followed him up the stairs, feeling as though her emotions had been tossed in a blender. Would he try to take Austin? Was he back for the rest of the summer? Had she ever held a place in his heart?

Outside the French doors, Hayden loomed before them and the alpenglow painted the Amphitheater a golden orange.

"Have a seat." He gestured to the green plastic lawn chair, the chaise long since returned to Gran.

"I prefer to stand, thank you." She latched on to the railing, her gaze trained on the view.

He moved beside her. "I have something for you." He held out a folded piece of paper that looked like a check.

She took hold, then opened it.

"Twenty-five thousand dollars!" Quickly scanning the sidewalk below, she prayed no one had heard her. She tempered her voice. "Are you crazy?"

"No more secrets, Blakely. Ross told me you're losing business."

"What? No, I'm not."

"You're not?" He looked surprised.

"No."

"But he said he offered to buy you out."

"Because Adventures in Pink is his stiffest competition. If anyone's in trouble, it's him." She refolded the check, this time in quarters and held it out to him. "So I don't need your money."

He pushed it away. "I owe you more than that in child support."

"Then put it in a college fund for Austin." She held it out again. "Like I said, I don't need your money, Trent."

He grabbed hold of the check along with her hand. "Then what do you need, Blakely?" He stepped closer.

She tried to tug free, but he held fast. "I don't need anything from you."

He took another step, eradicating what little space remained between them. "How about the truth? Why I didn't tell you I was leaving." His face was mere inches from hers.

She swallowed hard as the aroma of his aftershave invaded the space around her.

"Yes, I had commitments in Albuquerque. Yes, it was going to be hard to leave Austin. But then I realized I was in love with you. And let me tell you, sweetheart, you're one woman who's impossible to forget."

Her breathing intensified as his dark gaze bore into hers. If he thought she—

"I'm back, Blakely, and I'm back for good."

She struggled for air as his words rang in her mind. Back. For good? "What about your practice?"

"I've closed the door on my life in Albuquerque." He let go of her hand, only to seize her around the waist. "You and Austin are the only things that matter to me." He smoothed a lock of hair away from her face, his touch sending waves of pleasure throughout her being. "I love you, Blakely. And I don't care how long it takes—I intend to prove myself worthy of your trust."

She could melt into a puddle right there. If she weren't so stubborn. "What if I don't love you?"

He grinned. "Well then I'm just going to have to change your mind."

Before she could even form a response, he kissed her. A kiss filled with conviction and love. A kiss that erased any lingering doubt. She loved him.

If this was just the beginning, sign her up for a lifetime.

Epilogue

Blakely placed the lid on the last file box. The audit was complete and Adventures in Pink had passed with flying colors. More important, she survived, thanks to Granddad's impeccable record keeping…and Trent. The man was her rock, her best friend and the love of her life.

She lifted the white banker's box, carried it outside and placed it with the others in the bed of Trent's pickup. Tugging her cable-knit cardigan around her, she admired the shades of gold, orange and crimson that blanketed the mountainsides. Despite the midday sun, a chill had descended on the valley. Snow had already fallen in the higher elevations—enough to close both Black Bear and Imogene Pass. It appeared as though things were setting up for a long, hard winter.

"Are you ready, Mom?" Austin barreled around the pumpkin topiary situated at the corner of the blue building. Trent, who wasn't far behind their son, had a notable spring in his step. Thanks to the retirement of another doctor, Trent was now a permanent fixture at the clinic in Ridgway, and he loved every minute of it.

"You bet." She was a little taken aback by her son's enthusiasm. "But you do realize we're just going to the storage unit, right?"

"Yeah." He giggled as he opened the back door and crawled inside.

"He's in an exceptionally good mood today," she said as Trent moved to the passenger door. "You don't suppose he's got something up his sleeve do you?"

"Austin? Nah." Trent opened the door and waited while she climbed in. "Are you looking forward to our date tonight?"

"I am." What wasn't there to like when he whisked her away to Montrose for a romantic dinner? It was a rare event that made her feel special and gave her the opportunity to indulge her feminine side. "I even bought a new dress."

"Good." He leaned closer. "Because your legs are too amazing to keep hidden under jeans all the time."

Her cheeks flamed as he closed the door. Guess he'd approve of the high heels she got, too.

Trent fired up the engine and threw the truck into Reverse. "Say, would you mind if we made a little pit stop first?"

"No. What's up?"

"Oh, nothing." So he said, but that mischievous grin on his face told her otherwise.

But she didn't press him any further, opting instead to remain silent as he wound through the side streets of Ouray.

That is, until he drifted to a stop in front of a large Dutch Colonial built during the height of the gold rush. The home was beautiful, with its gabled dormers, large front porch and intricately carved woodwork; it also was one of Blakely's favorites. The one that had captivated her interest from the time she was a little girl when she and her mother would take walks around Ouray and daydream about the old homes.

"What are we doing here?"

Trent pulled the keys from the ignition. "I thought we might have a look-see."

"Cool." Austin bounded out of the backseat before she could get her door open.

She knew Trent had been looking for a house, but this…

"It's got four bedrooms—" Trent led them up the walk "—two and a half baths, and look at this yard. Plenty of room to play catch. Right, Austin?"

"Sure is." Their son hurried up the concrete steps.

"I've always admired the rounded bay windows." Blakely took in the structural elements.

"That's why I love these old homes. Builders nowadays don't pay attention to those small details that can really make a house stand out." Trent slid the key into the lock, then ushered them inside the empty house.

Dark, hand-scraped wood floors shimmered throughout the first level.

"All of the millwork is cherry and is original to the house." Trent shut the door and directed his attention to the living and dining rooms that flanked the foyer. "Of course it's been updated, so the kitchen cabinets are all new."

"Can I go upstairs?" Austin gripped the wood banister at the far end of the foyer.

"Sure. I expect you'll be spending a lot of time here, so you need to look at everything. May as well pick out a bedroom while you're up there." Trent motioned Blakely farther into the home as Austin thudded up the steps.

"Nice-size great room." She admired the beamed ceiling and stone fireplace. The rustic touches were a pleasant contrast to the formal rooms at the front of the house.

"Wait till you see this." He moved to one side, revealing the biggest kitchen she'd ever seen.

"Wow." Joining him, she smoothed her hand across the pale gold granite atop the island. Sage-green cupboards had a tea-stained glaze that not only highlighted their bead-board fronts, but also gave them an aged look. Like they'd been with the house all along. "Somebody did a good job selecting cabinets that held true to the character of the house."

"My thoughts exactly." Trent hadn't stopped grinning since they arrived.

Over the next forty-five minutes, he walked her through each room, showing her every detail of the magnificent structure. His excitement was hard to miss. However, she couldn't help thinking that this was a lot of house for a single guy.

Finally, they returned to the kitchen—definitely, her favorite room—while Austin continued to explore.

"Well, what do you think?"

"It's really nice, Trent. Really nice." In fact, the old house was every bit as beautiful on the inside as she'd imagined it to be from the outside.

"But…?"

She didn't want to hurt his feelings. "It's big. I mean, wouldn't you feel like you were rambling around?"

"I suppose." His gaze skimmed the great room. "It was definitely built with a family in mind." He paused. "So, I guess it's up to you."

"Me?" She stiffened.

Trent turned on his heel and dropped to one knee. Then, in what seemed like slow motion, he reached into his jacket pocket and smiled up at her. "I love you, Blakely Daniels. You are my treasure, and I want to spend the rest of my life with you. I want to fill this house with lots of kids. Our kids." He opened the black velvet box, revealing a brilliant princess-cut diamond surrounded by a halo of smaller diamonds. "Will you marry me?"

Afraid she might fall over, Blakely latched on to the island. Trent knelt before her, offering to make every dream she'd ever had come true. And oh, how she loved him.

Fighting back tears, she cleared the emotion from her throat. "When you say *lots* of kids—" she narrowed her gaze "—just how many are you talking about?"

He shrugged. "Two more. Ten more. Whatever you like."

She laughed. "I think ten would be a bit much. However… three might be just right."

He lifted a brow. "Is that a yes?"

"That is a resounding yes, Dr. Lockridge."

"All right!" Austin leaped down the stairs with a thud as Trent placed the ring on her left hand. "I told you she'd say yes, Dad."

"You knew about this?" Mouth agape, she looked at their son, knowing his dreams were coming true, as well.

He bounded toward them. "Uh-huh. So did Gran."

"And we pulled it off." Trent high-fived the boy and turned back to Blakely. His smoldering expression sent her heart into overdrive. "Now if you'll excuse me, son. I seriously need to kiss your mother."

Blakely wove her fingers through Trent's dark curls and tugged him closer. "I love you."

"Aw, man. Are you guys gonna do that all the time?"

She gazed into Trent's root beer eyes, so full of love for her and their family.

"I certainly hope so, short man. I certainly hope so."

* * * * *

Dear Reader,

I fell in love with Ouray, Colorado, the first time my mother-in-law introduced me to the small alpine town where her parents homesteaded in the 1920s. Located in southwestern Colorado, Ouray is known by many names—the Switzerland of America, the Gem of the Rockies, the Ice Climbing Capital of the U.S., and the Jeeping Capital of the World. The former silver and gold mining town is as rich in history as it is in beauty.

It was on my first hike up Portland Trail, as I stared out over the Amphitheater, that this story was conceived. In the years since, God has taught me that although things in life may not always go as I planned, all things really do work together for good. We hear that verse so often that it sometimes seems cliché. But, like Trent and Blakely, I've learned firsthand just how true it is. Life brings us hardships and we experience things that make absolutely no sense to our human minds. But beyond our comprehension, God is at work. While we're focused on that one piece of the puzzle, He sees the big picture and knows exactly how every piece fits together.

If you'd like to experience Ouray for yourself, Bob and Brandy Ross at Switzerland of America, the little blue building on Seventh Avenue, will be happy to set you up with a Jeep rental or take you on a scenic tour of the San Juan Mountains. And if you're in need of a place to stay, Ted and Betty Wolfe at the Comfort Inn will take good care of you. Just tell them all I sent you.

I hope you enjoyed *The Doctor's Family Reunion*, a story of trust, second chances and true love. Please feel free to contact me via my website, www.mindyobenhaus.com or you can snail mail me c/o Love Inspired Books, 233 Broadway, Suite 1001, New York, NY 10279.

Mindy Obenhaus

Questions for Discussion

1. In the story's opening, Blakely's world has been turned upside down—literally. Have you ever felt this way? How did you react?

2. Ross Chapman causes Blakely a lot of grief. Have you ever had someone in your life who was a thorn in your side? How did you deal with them?

3. Gran continued to pray for Trent because he was Austin's father, despite the fact that he'd hurt her granddaughter and married someone else. Have you ever felt led to pray for someone, regardless of circumstances?

4. Blakely's friend Taryn doesn't pull any punches. She is brutally honest with Blakely. Have you ever had a friend who wasn't afraid to be honest with you?

5. Trent achieved both of his dreams. Then he felt trapped. Have you ever had trouble trusting God?

6. Although Blakely worked with her grandfather for years, she found the administration side of Adventures in Pink overwhelming. Have you ever felt you've been given more than you can handle?

7. Blakely found herself pregnant and unwed at a young age, yet she made the choice to keep her baby. Have you ever known someone in that situation? What struggles did they face?

8. Although he never knew it, Blakely's grandfather affected Trent's life by being a godly example. Has there been anyone like that in your life? What did they mean to you?

9. Blakely had reserved one of her apartments to use as a studio, but she gave it up for Trent. Have you ever given up something that was important to you because you knew it was the right thing to do?

10. Trent signed off on the building with Scott because he was a man of his word, yet he felt God tugging him in another direction. Have you ever ignored God's calling? What happened?

11. Blakely was betrayed by Trent and hesitated to trust him again. Have you ever encountered a situation where you needed to take a second look at someone and learn to trust them again?